The Jekyll-Hyde
Murder Case

Tam
o' Shanter

The Jekyll-Hyde
Murder Case

MADELON ST. DENIS

COACHWHIP PUBLICATIONS
GREENVILLE, OHIO

The Author

Very little is known about the author, Madelon St. Denis. The use of 'St. Dennis' on her two traditionally published books appears to be a change by her publisher to accommodate marketing of those titles, as 'St. Denis' was often used on her magazine novels and foreign translations. 'St. Denis' is also how her name appears on a 1930 U.S. Census form, which notes she was born in 1885 in Massachusetts, and had been married at the age of 23. (She was 45 at the time of the census, lodging in New York.) One of her books, *The Death Kiss,* was made into a movie, so her name appears in conjunction with that in the 1930s, but she appears to have stopped writing by the end of the decade.

The Jekyll-Hyde Murder Case, by Madelon St. Denis
© 2024 Coachwhip Publications edition

First published Sept. 1930, *Complete Detective Novel Magazine*
CoachwhipBooks.com

ISBN 1-61646-581-6
ISBN-13 978-1-61646-581-0

1

The Fatal Dinner

"Careful, you fool! Can't you see it's murder?"

The speaker caught his companion's arm, restraining an impetuous forward movement.

"But—she may not be dead!"

"Of course she's dead, the fact's self-evident," the first speaker retorted. "Better dash up to the club and call the chief steward— Let him notify the local police, sheriff, or whoever's necessary, but see neither of you spreads the alarm. We don't want the whole herd tramping over the scenery. Hurry! I'll wait here."

When the younger man had started off at a long easy lope for the club house, the lights of which could be seen through intervening trees, Oakley Calhoun turned back to the rustic summer house and its strangely lit interior. He was careful not to cross the threshold, or to even touch the rough-barked arch that framed a scene as strange as any fantasy conjured by some sick or drunken brain. Yet his keen black eyes missed few of the perplexing details.

Someone had heaped dark-colored pillows against the further wall. And half on them, half against the rough wood of the wall itself, reclined a woman's body. That she was unmistakably dead, Calhoun felt no doubt. The stare of her wide, dark eyes was glassy as no living gaze could be. But the mere fact of death was but the beginning of the unforgettable picture.

Her slender white body was wrapped only in some gauzy, iridescent stuff, hardly thicker than a veil. Its soft folds clung to lovely tapering limbs and swirled in a silken nest about tiny bare feet, pathetically helpless in their still relaxation. Two tall, branched candelabra stood, one at either side of the dead woman, their burning candles bathing her in a golden light that struck answering gleams from her Saxon-yellow hair and picked out each item of the scene with mellow clearness.

In one ringed, white hand, were a few cards from a deck—the remainder of which had fallen, to scatter themselves, little blots of gaudy purple, over her body and the surrounding floor. The fingers of the other hand were curled around the stem of a fragile wine glass. But the crowning note of bizarre unreality was struck by a huge poinsettia flower that lay flame-red against her naked breast, seeming to spill its own crimson life in a narrow stream that flowed down her side, to form a small red pool.

Why? The question loomed, a sinister interrogation mark, in Oakley Calhoun's brain. Why the weird, elaborate stage set, the studied mockery of Death's solemn due?

"Is it meant to suggest an insane brain?"

The voice speaking at his shoulder might almost have been an answer, or a continuation of his own thoughts. He whirled, to find a girl or woman, he was hardly sure which, close beside him, her narrowed eyes fixed on the tragic tableaux revealed by the candle's mellow light.

"Now who the devil are you, and how'd you get here?" he demanded.

"No one you ever heard of." She tore her attention from the summer house long enough to favor him with a particularly winning smile. "Or at least, not unless you're interested in crimes and their solving. I happen to be a private detective known as Tam o' Shanter, and I'm staying at one of the near-by cottages."

"As a matter of fact, I have heard of you," he admitted. "Someone even pointed you out in the village. But that doesn't explain what you're doing in this remote part of the country club's grounds, and your costume shows you're not attending the dance."

"Not possible, since I wasn't invited," she good-naturedly retorted. "I was simply paddling about just off shore and enjoying the dance music, when I noticed how queerly this summer house was lit up. Naturally, being quite in the habit of indulging my curiosity, I beached the canoe and came up the bank to investigate."

"Any idea who she is?" A jerk of his head indicated the dead woman.

"Yes. I know her by sight as one of the club's social leaders, Leslie Carew."

"I feared as much!" His tone betrayed something that verged on regret. "Leslie Carew! I haven't seen her for years, in fact not since she married my best friend and started in squandering his millions. Wonder if she's really changed so much, or if it's the eerie setting?"

"Probably something of both. Have you sent for the coroner?"

"Was that the proper procedure? I didn't know, so I sent young Fitzharris for the club steward. Think they're coming now."

A group of half a dozen people were approaching through the trees, most of them carrying lanterns or flashlights, though the night was hardly dark enough to warrant their use. Oakley Calhoun went to meet them, Tam o' Shanter standing quietly in the shadow of the summer house.

"Careful, you fool! Can't you see
it's murder?"

The group stopped as he joined them and Owen Fitzharris hastily introduced his friend to a slight, distinguished-looking man, naming him as Carrol Ramsey, the district's coroner.

"Got hold of the head steward and he put me on to hunting up Dr. Ramsey and telling him what we'd found," Fitzharris explained. "The others are just incidentals, brought along to carry a stretcher and generally help out. We've kept the affair quiet and the club folks haven't an idea there's anything wrong."

"How did you two chance to discover the woman's body?" Dr. Ramsey asked, his eyes travelling curiously from one man to the other.

"We'd been driven out of doors by the heat and were strolling along the beach when the lights in the summer house made us think it was on fire. We naturally investigated and found—but you'd better have a look for yourself before the candles burn out."

He swung on his heel, heading back toward the summer house with Fitzharris and the coroner beside him. The others—Scanlan the head steward, two very much interested waiters carrying a stretcher, and a small grey-haired woman, one of the club stewardesses—trailed behind.

"God! It's Leslie Carew!" Ramsey cried out, as sight of the dead woman checked him on the threshold. "I'd have sworn she was among our dancers tonight!"

"Perhaps she was, earlier in the evening," Calhoun suggested. "But if so, what the devil has become of her clothes?"

"Leslie!" The coroner seemed stunned by discovery of the victim's identity. "To find her like this—it's ghastly— one of the proudest women alive! She'd have gone mad if she'd known her dead body was to be exposed to curious eyes like this! Only a fiend could dream of such a setting!"

"Does rather mock at what we're used to considering the dignity of death," Calhoun put in thoughtfully. "Do we have to leave her like that?"

"I'm afraid so. As coroner I have the right to examine her to make sure of her death, and its cause, but I can't disturb the scene until the police arrive; they'd insist I had destroyed valuable clues."

"City or village police?"

"Neither, we're outside the village limits so come under the jurisdiction of the State Constabulary. I've phoned them. They may see fit to call in the New York Homicide Bureau."

Slowly, with evident reluctance, he stepped inside the summer house and bent over Leslie Carew's lovely, almost naked body. His fingers lifted the sprawling poinsettia flower, to show beneath it an ugly little round hole which pierced the white breast directly above her heart and was the origin of the crimson stream that had seemed to flow from the flower itself.

"Shot, of course, and from some little distance—there are no powder marks. Anybody found the weapon?"

Inquisitive eyes searched the floor. Scanlan, the club steward, even flashed his light into shadowy corners of the little place, but there was no sign of a pistol.

"That was one reason I told Fitzharris not to spread the alarm; the fewer people who tramp over the grass tonight the more we may hope to read from it by daylight."

"There seems to be something hidden under her feet."

Coroner Ramsey turned quickly at sound of the new voice, to find Tam o' Shanter idly lounging in the arched entrance, hands deep in her sweater pockets and narrowed, smoke-blue eyes intently studying the corpse.

"Miss O'Brien!" He hailed her appearance with evident relief. "What lucky spirit sent you along?"

"Only the little gods of chance. Can I help at all?"

"You most certainly can," he emphatically declared. "I'm more or less at sea; we're not in the habit of having murders around here and I haven't an idea of exactly what should be done, while all this is an old story to you."

"Perhaps the fact of the victim's being a friend rather puts you off your stride, also the strangeness of the setting someone's been at such pains to arrange. Suppose, first of all, you see what's under her feet. Of course we shouldn't touch it, but there's a bit of something white—paper, I think—you can pull it clear out without really disturbing her."

Ramsey unhesitatingly followed her advice, stooping to gently withdraw an oblong piece of white paper which had been almost completely hidden under the bare feet and swirl of silken gauze. He held it up to the light with a muttered word of perplexity; only a roughly cut oblong of white wrapping paper on which was a printed series of numbers: "997033"—nothing else.

"Does it mean anything?" He appealed rather helplessly to Tam's wider experience of crime.

"It must, otherwise it wouldn't be here, for there's no chance of its having been accidentally dropped; it was quite evidently placed under her feet by set purpose. But as to what it means—" Her slim shoulder climbed with a movement almost Latin in its sluffing of all opinion whatsoever. "It's too early to hazard even a guess."

The coroner laid the paper down close to Leslie Carew's feet, making no effort to replace it beneath them, then straightened to address the club steward.

"Do you know if Mrs. Carew was at the club house tonight?"

"She was, sir, I saw her myself early in the evening."

"You're positive?"

"Certainly, sir. I've good reason to remember, for Mrs. Carew was a most particular lady, and she called me into the private room she'd engaged for a supper party, to find fault with its arrangement."

"Oh, so she gave a supper party tonight? Who were her guests?"

"As to that I can't say, sir. Being particularly busy with the dance, I turned seeing to her over to Mrs. Snell here. She can tell you more as to what happened."

At a sign from the coroner the little grey-haired stewardess, who had been lingering unobtrusively in the background, reluctantly drifted forward, taking care not to approach the body on the pillows too closely.

"You attended to Mrs. Carew's supper party, Dorcas?" He evidently knew her by sight and name.

"Yes, sir; that is, I saw to the setting of the table and the flowers, and had Leon, one of our waiters, put the food on the sideboard—Mrs. Carew wanted no service."

"No service?" Ramsey echoed. "Why was that?"

"I don't quite know, sir. But there was something queer about the whole party."

"In what way?"

"Well, to begin with, Mrs. Carew telephoned the order reserving a dining room to Mr. Scanlan, and he either made a mistake in the number of guests or she afterwards changed her mind—at least she was very annoyed at finding four places set when she wanted only two. She gave him rather a bad time about it."

"So you removed the two extra places?"

"Yes, sir, and took her order about the cold supper to be placed on the sideboard where they could help themselves. She was very particular about none of us disturbing them; I even heard her lock the door leading into the hall after I'd seen that Leon had everything to her liking."

"But if the door was locked how was this solitary guest of hers expected to get in?"

"Through the French window, I imagine, sir. That dining room has one opening on the side terrace."

"Mrs. Carew didn't mention the name of her guest?"

"Oh, no, sir!" Dorcas appeared to consider the question as a pitiful example of masculine stupidity. "The whole meeting was most certainly meant to be kept a secret, otherwise why should she be so particular on not having even a waiter in the room, once the food had been placed in readiness? She was not a lady who usually liked waiting on herself."

"No, I suppose not," Ramsey thought, fully conceded. "And so you caught no glimpse of the mysterious guest?"

"As to that, well—I'd hardly like to say."

"Exactly what do you mean?" He regarded the quiet little woman with an even deeper interest; she seemed in the way of proving herself their star witness.

"It was like this, sir." She twirled a bit of her skirt between thin, nervous fingers. "Of course I had no thought of spying on Mrs. Carew, but just happening to be at the further end of the side terrace I saw a tall woman in a flame-colored dress slip in through the French window of Number 14—the room occupied by Mrs. Carew."

"What time was this?"

"A few minutes after nine, sir."

"You think she was the expected guest?"

"No, I don't sir!" Dorcas respectfully contradicted. "It was only a few minutes after nine, and Mrs. Carew had let out her guest wasn't due until nearly ten."

"How did she do that?"

"By glancing at her wrist-watch, sir, and asking if the salad would keep crisp until ten o'clock."

"I see. So you think this lady in red was an unlooked for incident? You didn't 'just happen' to see her leave?"

Dorcas slightly reddened at his tone; she was evidently sensitive on the subject of spying.

"No, sir, though I do think I saw the same lady later on in a roadster that drove away from one of the side entrances —I'd not like to say for certain, but her dress was an odd, very bright red—I saw no other to match it all evening."

"You don't know, or suspect, if it was anyone known to you?"

"Indeed no, sir, I only saw her frock and nicely-dressed dark hair, black I should think. But—" She hesitated, then decided to take the plunge. "There's one other thing I might say, though I don't know if it has anything to do with what's happened— Mrs. Carew and this lady in red seemed to be quarrelling very violently; I heard their two voices raised as I was going by the door of Number 14 at about quarter past nine. And one of the voices, I'm not sure which, was fairly screaming."

"It begins to look as if the explanation of tonight's tragedy might lie in whatever occurred in Room 14," Ramsey remarked, his fine brows drawn into a perplexed knot. "Pity, Dorcas, that you weren't hovering as closely around the room when, and after, Mrs. Carew's supper guest actually arrived."

"I'm always very busy when there's a dance going on, sir. I had no time," Dorcas primly explained, thereby tacitly admitting that it was time and not inclination which had been lacking.

"Well, what you did see and hear is likely to prove immensely useful." The coroner consoled her. "I hope Room 14 is just as Mrs. Carew left it—that it hasn't been cleared or anything disturbed?"

"I don't think it's been so much as entered, sir; we've all had our hands full tonight."

Here Tam, who had been quietly listening, volunteered her services. "Why not let me examine the room, and watch that no one tampers with it, while you're waiting for the police?"

"Good idea!" Ramsey cordially assented. "Your faculty of observation is better trained than mine, and you'll see clues I'd almost certainly miss; in fact, it would be a great relief if you'd agree to help me out on the entire case."

"Let's leave that until later." Such was Tam's noncommittal reply, as her eyes travelled rapidly over the assembled group, finally settling on Oakley Calhoun. "If you're a member or guest of the club, Mr. Calhoun, I'd be glad if you'd go with me; I may have trouble in getting admitted unless there's someone to vouch for me."

"I have a guest-membership card," he declared, "and I'll be more than grateful at being allowed to tag along and watch your methods."

2

Tam Uses Her Eyes

"I asked you along partly to extract all the information you possess about the Carews," Tam frankly informed him as they walked in the direction of the club—from which gay dance music was still issuing, despite the lateness of the hour; almost two o'clock.

"Alas! Another hope blasted!" Calhoun lamented. "I quite thought you'd discerned my unusual intelligence and meant using it in the cause of justice."

"It's entirely on the cards that I may do just that," she retorted. "Depends on what symptoms of ability the next hour calls forth." Then with an abrupt settling to business: "Did I understand you to say you hadn't seen Leslie Carew since she was first married?"

"Not later than the first year of her marriage." He slightly qualified his former statement. "But it wasn't because of any estrangement between her husband, Eric Carew, and me—I've simply been almost continuously out of the country since then, and have missed seeing her for one reason or another during the few times I've been back."

"Will you resent my asking if the marriage was a happy one?"

"You've heard rumors to the contrary?"

"Yes."

"Probably no harm in admitting that it wasn't. I suppose the fact's common knowledge, since Eric ended—a suicide."

"I'd heard that fact hinted at," Tam acknowledged. "Two or three years ago, wasn't it?"

"Just under three. Their son was little more than a baby; he must be about six now."

"You haven't seen him?"

"No, purposely kept away because my feeling toward the woman who'd ruined Eric's life was none too kindly. Besides, I've only been back a couple of weeks, and only two days here in Meadow Dale as the guest of Owen Fitzharris. I wasn't aware that the Carews ever lived in this vicinity."

"They've a wonderful estate, one of the show places of Long Island—or rather her father, Mr. Lord, has," Tam informed him. "I've seen it, also the Carew baby; he's an adorable tot." They had almost reached the club house when she added: "You knew her engagement to Truxton Manning, the wealthy oil man, had just been announced?"

"No, I hadn't heard that!"

"It was in Sunday's paper. Sorry, now, that I only glanced at the article—I never imagined one of our social leaders was about to become the crux of a murder case. Here we are; I'll let you arrange about getting into Room 14."

Oakley Calhoun was one of those men who seldom experience much difficulty in getting things in general arranged to suit him; perhaps his long sojourn in China and other parts of the Orient had given him the habit of command. Tam, watching the ease with which he obtained admission to the still locked private dining room, was conscious of a strong inclination to annex him as unofficial assistant—for the duration of the present case at least.

Number 14 was a small, luxuriously fitted dining room. Its carved refectory table, barely large enough to accommodate four diners, was at present laid with places for only two, and it was this table which first absorbed Tam's attention to the momentary exclusion of everything else. She studied the various dishes and glasses, noted their arrangement and the lay of forks and knives—her eyes narrowed and darkened to a chill grey, with no hint of the sunnier blue that flecked them at happier moments.

Calhoun, more acutely interested in this attractive girl detective, for whom Dr. Ramsey seemed to entertain a marked respect, than in the room or what it could tell them, watched her until she looked up to encounter his faintly quizzical smile.

"I know, as a layman you think I'm wasting too much time simply looking," she accused. "You'd prefer seeing me crawl round the floor with a yard stick and magnifying glass. But how to look is one of the first things a detective needs to learn—have you any idea how little most people really see what they look at?"

"Never thought about it," he confessed.

"Of course not, nobody does." Then, with a hint of tartness in her voice. "Just to prove how dormant the faculty of observation is in most people, even intelligent people, suppose you tell me how much this supper table reveals to you."

"Why—" His handsome black eyes lighted with a touch of whimsical amusement. "It surely hasn't much to tell—only that two people have supped off lobster-mayonnaise with a few extras, and shared a bottle of wine."

"Nothing else?"

Calhoun cast an appraising eye over the table. "They smoked, of course, but that doesn't mean anything nowadays; everybody does."

"And that's all you see?" Her tone was scornful.

"Have I missed any enlightening details?"

"Oh, a trifle or two," Tam jeered, "For instance, that one of the diners (presumably Mrs. Carew, since the cigarette stubs at that place are gold tipped, scented, extremely expensive and stained with lip rouge of the same general tint as that now decorating her dead lips) never ate her salad at all. She merely poked at it with her fork enough to soil the tips of the prongs, but not enough to show it had been used to lift even one real mouthful. Still, she smoked eleven gold-tipped cigarettes, and she either drank several cups of coffee or took it inordinately sweet, for the sugar container is almost empty. And her guest took no coffee at all; that cup hasn't been used."

"So—and the other diner, presumably the guest?" Calhoun demanded with thoroughly awakened interest.

"He or she, we don't at present know which, must have been ravenously hungry—that plate and the salad bowl on the serving table are both empty. The former has even been wiped off with a piece of bread, and you'll notice the rolls are all gone, also there's not much doubt who ate them, as the butter knife we've tentatively assigned to Mrs. Carew hasn't been touched."

"From which facts you deduce—"

He prompted.

"It's too early for decided opinions," Tam hedged. "But from the indications I rather think Mrs. Carew's supper engagement was hardly a welcome one—something in the nature of an obligation, or duty, rather than a pleasure; it seems to have robbed her of appetite and driven her to nervous indulgence in too many cigarettes and too much black coffee."

"You don't consider it a love tryst, then? By the bye, where is this man she was engaged to?"

"Truxton Manning? Out on the west coast, visiting some of his oil fields—or at least so the Sunday paper stated, though of course it may not be true."

"You haven't answered my first question," he reminded her.

"Concerning a possible love tryst? I scarcely know. That might easily explain the lady's loss of appetite; love does quaint things to most of my sex. But it hardly accounts for the guest's frankly betrayed hunger—one rather expects more restraint, or deceit, in a lover. And there's another puzzling item, which I suppose you haven't noticed—the ash tray at the place we're considering as the guest's holds two gold-tipped butts and three of a very cheap brand. Now, I wonder why?"

"Rather suggests the guest may have been of a different social class."

"So you *can* use your imagination, once it's actually stirred up!" Tam grinned at him with a boy-like friendliness. "That's precisely how it struck me—friend guest evidently carried his, or her, own smokes, of a decidedly inferior grade, and was only offered, or accepted, two of the hostess' expensive brand."

She slowly moved around the table, scrutinizing it from the opposite side so that the shaded lights struck across the damask at a different angle.

"Ah!" The small ejaculation told of dissatisfaction. "There's a flaw somewhere in my reasoning—shows how fatal it is to trust snap judgments."

"What's wrong now?" Calhoun regarded the table with open bewilderment.

"You've surely noticed how often a person who's nervous or absent-minded draws designs or initials on any convenient surface?" She glanced up to receive his assenting nod, then went on. "Whoever sat in the place we've assigned to the guest marked initials on the cloth with a knife, or possibly a spoon edge and—they look like 'L. C.'!"

She reached for the pepper-shaker and lightly scattered some of its black grains over the scrawled initials, then very gently blew most of them away, leaving only those that had settled in the marked indentations. They unmistakably formed the letters "L.C.," repeated five or six times.

"All your nice deductions about their appetites gone galley-west!" Calhoun chuckled delightedly. "Leslie must have sat there."

"Not certain," she retorted, making a quick dash at the sideboard, where her trained eyes had caught a signed supper cheque; once it was spread on the table and the name boldly dashed across the bottom compared with the letters on the table cloth, it was Tam's turn to wax triumphant, for both the "L." and "C." were totally different. "All the same, it's odd," she commented. "Why should the guest mark Mrs. Carew's initials instead of his, or her own? All wrong, Mr. Calhoun—distinctly wrong and dead against the precepts of applied psychology! Well, let's see if the room holds any more contradictions."

She commenced a search, which, to the watching Calhoun seemed rather casual, until he noticed how her lithely bending body brought every section of the thick carpet under her eyes as she sauntered about, never actually stooping, but swaying down toward the floor and up again with an effortless ease that told of perfectly trained muscles perfectly conditioned. Finally she swooped into one of the further corners, then displayed a tiny wire hairpin on her extended palm.

"Black, so it never belonged to gold-haired Leslie Carew—but I'm not at all sure it was dropped tonight. The state of the carpet suggests the room hasn't been swept for a week; either that, or several people have positively tramped about, for the thick pile is crushed down in the most unexpected places."

She was still intently examining the room when Owen Fitzharris came to report progress.

"The State police are here, a sergeant and two troopers," he announced. "Also a police photographer and finger-print expert. They're all busy at the summer house. This room's to be locked and left untouched till morning."

"Does Dr. Ramsey want me?" Tam asked.

"No, he sent word you'd better go home and snatch a few hours' sleep—the grounds adjoining the summer house are to be searched at dawn; suppose he thought you'd want to be present."

"Surely." She nodded half absently, part of her atten-tion being held by sounds of the breaking up of the club dance; soft laughter, voices calling for cars, the whir of hastily started motors. "I wonder if it wouldn't have been wiser to make inquiries among the dancers?" she meditat-ed aloud. "We might at least have found someone who saw the woman in red."

"But it was you who first suggested not spreading the alarm," Fitzharris reminded her.

"Yes, at first we didn't want the lawn and bank walked over. But surely, now the State police are here, the crowd could be kept off. What's to be done with Mrs. Carew's body? And has her family been told?"

"She's to be taken up to Dune House," Fitzharris an-swered. "And the coroner's gone ahead to break the news to her father."

When room 14 had been carefully locked, Tam retain-ing possession of the key, both men insisted on escorting her home, since the hour was unconscionably late, or more accurately, early.

"You're not one of the regular colony?" Calhoun asked, with a half guilty realization that the young detective and her concerns were absorbing much more of his thoughts than the tragic death of his best friend's beautiful widow.

"Heavens, no. I came here strictly on business; the matter of a jewel robbery, and once that was closed up I only stayed on to enjoy a few days' swimming. I meant leaving tomorrow or the day after, though Dr. Ramsey's asking me to work with him on this case may cause a change of plans."

"You seem to know the doctor rather well," Calhoun put in with just the faintest hint of resentment.

"Yes, it was he who persuaded a friend into engaging me to recover his lost gems; we've more or less known each other for years, through his friendship for the district attorney and one or two of the higher police officials."

"I noticed he seemed to think your sudden appearance providential."

"Well, I've had more experience of murder cases than he has," Tam defended her old friend's attitude. "Being a coroner in a section like Meadow Dale doesn't entail much actual work. Here we are." They neared a cozy, honeysuckle-covered cottage. "Thanks so much for seeing me home—I hope my landlady is peacefully sleeping, otherwise she'll begin thinking me one of the fast set she so abhors. Good-night, or rather good-morning!"

She slipped silently through the cottage gate and disappeared under the vine- hung little porch.

"How do you suppose a girl like that ever came to be a detective?" Oakley Calhoun ruminated aloud as the two friends retraced their steps along the now deserted country road.

"No telling what a girl may fancy doing in these emancipated times; besides, I imagine the work's fascinating."

"Maybe so. But only think of the criminal types she must match wits against—a girl like that! A lady! God, it's awful!"

"Waxing sentimental in your old age" Fitzharris jeered. "Sheltered and protected life for women, and all that rot? Don't you realize most of 'em don't want protection?"

Calhoun merely snorted resentfully and scorned an answer.

Once in her own immaculate cottage bedroom, Tam slowly undressed, her mind busy with the strange problem unfolded during the past few hours. Who had killed the petted, ultra-fashionable young widow, and why? Above all, what design lay behind the fantastic setting in the summer house? Once that was known the rest would prove plain sailing, she believed; but what conceivable explanation other than that of a diseased brain could cover such bizarre details as the almost naked, gauze-draped body— the lighted candles, scattered cards and empty wine glass? As for the poinsettia flower, that might easily have come from Room 14; Tam had noticed the same gaudy blossoms used as decorations there, though there seemed no sensible reason why it should have been arranged to cover the deadly little bullet hole while at the same time numerous candles were lighted, apparently to call prompt attention to the summer house and its tragic contents.

Where had the candles come from, she wondered; where was the murder-weapon and what had become of the victim's clothes? Her brain fairly bristled with unanswered questions until, with the determination born of long practice, she swept it clean of thoughts and stretched between the cool sheets, her will firmly set on gaining at least a few hours' needed sleep.

Even then, just before the desired oblivion closed around her, the vision of a white oblong bearing the numbers "997033" hovered hazily above her closed lids.

What was its meaning?

3

Mrs. Sarah Carew

Early as Tam arrived on the scene of last night's tragedy, she found the State Troopers already at work. They were systematically covering every inch of the short thick grass, hunting for the death weapon or any other clue they might discover.

"Found the pistol used?" Tam called to the nearest trooper.

He glanced at her, then saluted with a pleasant smile; strangers were apt to fancy Tam on sight.

"No, Miss, and no sign of the lady's clothes," he answered. "But we came across her hand bag over there to the left—the coroner has it."

"Where is he?"

"Up at the club house, Miss. He left word, he'd like you to come up there—that is, if you're Miss O'Brien."

"I am, and thanks for the message."

She stood watching them for a moment longer, then walked up to the club, where she found Dr. Ramsey enjoying a cup of early coffee on a side terrace.

"Morning, Miss O'Brien—won't you join me?"

He looked utterly fatigued and was still wearing his last night's dinner clothes. Coffee being one of Tam's pet weaknesses, she promptly accepted, in spite of having already breakfasted at the cottage.

"You haven't been to bed," she accused.

"No, I haven't even taken time to change," he admitted. "Leslie's father, Mr. Lord, was so hideously upset that I hated leaving him. And there were a thousand things to do; among others we went through her private papers, hoping to find some sort of clue." He paused, to thoughtfully sip his fragrant coffee.

"And did you?" Tam prompted.

"I hardly know—one hesitates to connect a woman with murder. Do you happen to know Rosamond Forbes?"

"Isn't she the striking-looking widow, or divorcee, who owns a place called The Willows?"

"Yes. She's a divorcee, and by her husband's act, not her own."

"I've been too busy over that jewel robbery that brought me here to pick up much gossip about the residents who weren't directly concerned in my case. But I have heard it whispered that Mrs. Forbes was considered rather outside the social pale."

"Something of the sort's been going on—woman's work; of course, we men would hardly condemn Rosamond—a few indiscretions are almost permissible in a woman whose husband treats her as Rosamond's did. Mrs. Carew, Leslie's mother-in-law, tells me it was Leslie who used her position as social dictator to close other women's doors against Rosamond Forbes."

"Good women are apt to be merciless to others who've been careless enough to get found out," Tam remarked. "Has this social ostracism any connection with the murder?"

"Just possibly—that's what I'm uncertain about," He drew some papers from an inner coat pocket and selecting one, a letter, handed it to her. "Read that—we found it among Leslie's papers," It was written in an emotional sort of script on highly scented paper, and began abruptly:

"Leslie:—How dare you deliberately shut every door in my face? The Meadow Dale women follow you like so many sheep and you're taking advantage of that fact to render my position impossible—I've even been given the deliberate cut by some of your stodgy followers.

"If you think I intend tolerating such treatment you're wrong! I shall be at the club dance tonight, even if you have seen to it that I received no invitation, and I mean forcing you into changing your attitude, or else teaching you to damn well repent it!

Rosamond Forbes."

"H-m-m! The lady evidently feels aggrieved, not to say resentful!" Tam commented as she returned the letter. "Still, that's hardly an adequate motive for murder."

"I'm not so sure," His tone was decidedly worried. "Knowing Rosamond rather well, I can't forget that she's always owned a fiendish temper. She once beat a housemaid for smashing some bit of cherished bric-a-brac, so severely that the girl dragged her into court and collected damages. Also she physically answers Dorcas' description of the woman who slipped into Room 14—she's tall and black-haired, and furthermore one of the men who had charge of the parking arrangements last night declares Rosamond was here in a roadster, and wearing a flame-colored evening gown."

"Surely Dorcas said she had seen this woman in red driving away from the club quite early in the evening," Tam objected.

"I know, but she may have come back. Besides, we've no proof as to where and at what exact moment Leslie was actually killed; it may have been in Room 14 and her body afterwards carried to the summer house."

"Through a throng of club guests and attendants?" One of Tam's level dark eyebrows climbed into a skeptical arch. "And I've been pretty thoroughly over the supper room; there's not a trace of blood anywhere."

"Still, the two women could have met later on in the grounds," Ramsey persisted. "Suppose, after the quarrel that Dorcas overheard in the supper room, Rosamond drove away, then started brooding over her own social wrongs, growing more and more furious until she finally worked herself into such a state that she came back thirsting for vengeance."

"Doesn't sound convincing," Tam demurred, "though possibly I underrate the strength of feeling such social ostracism might arouse."

"More than probably. Living an interesting, active life such as yours, it's difficult to realize how much an accepted position means to women who have nothing but Society—spelled with a distinct capital 'S'—to make life worth living. Rosamond may have reasoned, if she was not enraged past reasoning at all, that once Leslie's influence was removed the rest would take her back into the fold."

"Please don't think me stubborn; I simply can't really accept your theory."

"Well, it's hardly tangible enough to be called that— merely the ghost of a shadow of suspicion." He smiled with tired friendliness as he offered his cigarette case and took one himself. "At present we seem so utterly bankrupt of other possible suspects. One of the State Troopers found Leslie's bag, and its contents seem intact—also it's a valuable thing of itself—so robbery can't have been the motive."

"I noticed her rings hadn't been taken."

"Oh, one puzzling thing was discovered after you and Mr. Calhoun left the summer house last night. On lifting the body, we found perhaps half a cup full of a rather coarse white substance scattered under it, on both floor and pillows. What do you suppose it was?"

"Naturally I've no idea."

"Granulated sugar!" Ramsey shot out the words with disgusted impatience. "Now, what, in the name of common sense, was it doing there?"

"No more fantastic than the other details," Tam quietly asserted. "Yet I believe, when we reach the final solution, we'll find a reason behind every one—that is, of course, unless they were scattered haphazard to create an impression of insanity."

"You lean toward that explanation?"

"Frankly, I don't. I'm more inclined to suspect motive behind the seeming medley. But I may later on change that opinion. The pistol used hasn't come to light?"

"Not yet. I left word I was to be told immediately if they found it. I'm afraid the murderer took it away. Too bad the grass is so well kept all around the summer house—it gives us nothing at all in the way of footprints."

"And her clothes? A modern evening outfit wouldn't make a very large parcel, but do you think they were also carried away by the murderer?"

"Lord, I've not yet reached the stage of really thinking! My brain's still spinning round in dazed circles. Did you learn anything special from the supper room?"

"I found only this." She produced and gave him the tiny black invisible hairpin, then launched into a brief summary of her conclusions drawn from dishes and silver, ending: "Do you know if Leslie Carew did smoke gold-tipped cigarettes?"

"Never anything else," he affirmed. "And highly scented ones at that—I heard half a dozen men friends reproach her for execrable taste on their account. Oh, by the way, I forgot to mention that Mrs. Carew says the rainbow scarf wrapped around Leslie's body was part of her own evening frock, the one she wore last night. That gauzy stuff was draped over an undergarment of some silvery cloth, so Mrs. Carew declares."

"I know, with those long flowing lines so much in vogue now." Tam nodded wisely, "It takes yards and yards to produce that effect. Poor woman, what a ghastly use to put her own fripperies to! I think her murderer must have hated her."

"Don't they always?" Ramsey inquired on a note of surprise.

"Usually, perhaps, not always. It's sometimes only a spurt of uncontrollable rage or jealousy, which after all holds a certain element of love. And outside of those passions, murder is often motivated by deliberate intention to remove a troublesome obstacle—with no really personal animosity for the victim. Here comes one of the troopers; let's hope they've found the missing gun."

But the approaching trooper had nothing quite so important to offer. He had only found a tiny spray of diamond-set flowers, evidently broken from a piece of jewelry. Dr. Ramsey turned it curiously this way and that, then handed it over for Tam's feminine inspection.

"They're real stones," she almost instantly decided. "And it must have formed part of some quite handsome ornament. A brooch, I think, or possibly a bracelet; the shape doesn't suggest a usual design of either ear or finger rings."

"There were no other pieces anywhere near it?" Ramsey inquired.

"No, sir, I looked carefully; this bit was twenty feet or more from the summer house."

"Had it lain long where you found it?" Tam asked him. "I mean, was it embedded in the earth or lying lightly on the surface?"

"Lightly, Miss; it hadn't even worked through the grass roots to the solid ground."

"You think we're justified in taking it for granted it was dropped last night on the scene of the crime?" Ramsey asked her when the trooper had gone back toward the summer house.

"Tentatively, yes. You'll remember we had a hard shower around three yesterday afternoon—that would have beaten the spray into the earth if it had lain there then. I wonder if it was broken from any piece of jewelry belonging to Leslie Carew? If not, we'd be justified in assuming the presence of another woman near the summer house, though whether or not her hand fired the fatal shot remains an open question."

"I'm going up to Dune House as soon as I've stolen time for a shave and changed into other clothes—suppose you accompany me?" Ramsey suggested. "I'd like you to meet Leslie's father, also her mother-in-law, and the latter can surely tell us if those little flowers came from anything Leslie wore."

While the coroner freshened after his night's arduous activities, Tam strolled through the club's various halls and lounging rooms, with no particular object other than a general quest for useful or enlightening scraps of information that might be collected through friendly gossip with any of the club's employees. She saw nothing of Scanlan or Dorcas, the only two whom she already knew by sight, but presently encountered a pleasant-faced stewardess who, realizing Tam was a stranger, asked if she was looking for anyone.

"No, just waiting for Dr. Ramsey, who's promised to take me up to Dune House."

"Really, Miss?" The woman was instantly all interest. "Might I ask if you're in the way of being a newspaper reporter?"

"Nothing like that!" Tam answered with her most Irish and confidence-inspiring smile. "I only happened to be one of the first to discover last night's dreadful tragedy."

"Oh, and wasn't it an awful thing, Miss!" The plump hands were thrown aloft as if calling the higher powers to witness. "They do say the poor young lady had nothing on whatsoever, and was fair reeking in blood!"

"Neither's at all true," Tam assured her. "But you know how people will exaggerate, especially when the victim is such a wealthy, popular person as Leslie Carew."

"Indeed they will, Miss, and small wonder, her being known to everybody as she was, and that open handed— It's a great loss to the club, Miss, a great loss, and I'm thinking there's only one person hereabouts as will be glad."

"Now, that amazes me!" Tam was all respect for the other's superior knowledge. "How could such a lovely woman have enemies?"

"It's often in one's own household they spring up, Miss," was the stewardess' dark response. "Such as a mother by marriage, Miss—though I'd not want to be mentioning any names." And with that, apparently rather frightened by her own temerity, the woman muttered some transparent excuse and vanished toward forbidden service regions.

Half an hour later, as Dr. Ramsey drove toward Dune House, Tam asked if he had ever heard any rumors of friction between Mrs. Carew and her son's widow.

"Being known as a close friend of the family, whispers of that sort wouldn't be likely to reach my ears," he answered. "On the other hand, I think, from personal observation, that the elder Mrs. Carew has always more or less blamed Leslie for Eric's suicide. Both women were too well bred ever to allow a hint of discord to mar the surface smoothness of their family life—but I've sometimes thought only devotion to her small grandson kept Sarah Carew an inmate of the house. Ever since Eric's death she has lived practically a recluse, seldom attending any but the most informal family dinners, and never going into society at all."

"She must be rather an interesting type. I'm quite anxious to see her," Tam declared. Nor was she disappointed in the actual meeting with Mrs. Sarah Carew, whose strangely immobile face and great haunted eyes gave her the look of some ancient priestess of a gloomy creed; an impression her trailing garments of unrelieved black did nothing to remove.

"Mr. Lord will be here in a moment." Mrs. Carew's voice was unexpectedly deep, almost masculine in timbre, and the saddest Tam had ever heard.

Dr. Ramsey took out and displayed the diamond-set scroll of platinum. "This was found not far from the summer house. Do you know if it's broken from any piece of jewelry Leslie owned?"

"I think not." She held it between long, thin fingers, much as one might hold some objectionable insect. "But Anice, Leslie's maid, can tell you positively—she naturally knows her mistress' ornaments better than I do."

When her ring was answered by a footman he sent for Anice, who presently entered the big drawing-room, looking pathetically small and ill at ease. Tam noticed that the girl's eyes were red, as if she had been crying. She unhesitatingly denied her dead mistress ownership of the broken spray, declaring she was well acquainted with all the younger Mrs. Carew's ornaments, and that this piece matched none of them. Then, that point settled, she lingered, unheeding or perhaps not seeing Mrs. Carew's gesture of dismissal, until Dr. Ramsey asked if there was anything she wished to tell them.

"It's only about some money, sir. I don't know if Mrs. Carew's evening bag was found," the girl apologized.

"It was," he told her, "and its contents seem to be untouched. There were several valuable articles, a gold compact, a cigarette case and a little filigree purse containing a trifle over fifty dollars in bills and silver."

"But there's no roll of bigger bills, with an elastic around them?" Anice gasped.

"No! Are you sure the bag held anything of that kind?"

"It did when she left home, sir," Anice asserted. "Yesterday morning she sent me to cash a cheque for two thousand dollars—at the bank in the village, you know, sir—and I saw her crowd the money into her evening bag just before starting for the dance!"

"Then the money's gone, and the fact that she carried so much rather changes the aspect of things. Was there anything else you wanted to tell us, Anice?"

"No, sir, nothing else." And the girl slipped away, but not before Tam's observant eyes had caught her timid side glance at Mrs. Carew; it suggested that there was some further information which she longed to impart, but dared not because of the older woman's presence.

"Does blackmail explain the unusual secrecy of last night's supper party?" Dr. Ramsey inquired of no one in particular. "Two thousand rolled up with an elastic around it—I wonder what's become of that money?"

"The fact that she had it adds another reason why we need to learn the identity of her supper guest," Tam cut in. "Surely someone must have seen the guest either entering or leaving Room 14! I'm afraid we'll have to fine comb all the club employees and all those who attended the dance."

Here Leslie Carew's father came in carrying an open telegram, and the subject of the missing money was temporarily dropped.

"A wire's just come from Truxton Manning," Mr. Lord informed them. "His lawyer finally located him in Chicago, on his way back from the west coast, and he says he's arranging to fly from there to New York, arriving sometime this afternoon or evening. Poor man, it's a terrible home-coming for him."

Did Tam see, or only imagine, a gleam of exultant triumph that flashed for a second in Sarah Carew's great mournful eyes, to be instantly hidden under thick drooped lids?

Tam swam until she found the
murder gun—on the bottom. Now
she felt she could make progress

4

"We Quarreled"

Oakley Calhoun sentineled a small knoll in the club ground smoking a dissatisfied cigarette and watching a solitary feminine bather just off the point on which the rustic summer house was built.

The day, suddenly cloudy, had turned cool and there was only this one erratic swimmer in the water, apparently bent on giving the closest possible human imitation of a sportive seal.

Calhoun strolled nearer and presently took out his watch, admiringly timing the length of the summer's frequent disappearances under water. He had gained a position almost directly inshore from the girl when she suddenly came to the surface and struck toward the beach, swimming easily on her side with some dark object clutched in her left hand. As she reached the shallow water, straightened, and unexpectedly waved to him he saw that it was Tam o' Shanter, the girl detective for whom he had vainly searched all morning. She caught up a long bathing cape, wrapping it around her as she rapidly climbed the steep sandy shore.

"I've found it!" She called out with a touch of triumph and proudly displayed a small but deadly-looking little pistol.

"In the water?" He asked rather stupidly, and was promptly laughed at.

"Naturally—you didn't suppose I took it in swimming with me?"

"Why hunt for it all by yourself like that?"

"Everyone else is busy—Dr. Ramsey performing the autopsy, the State Troopers trying to locate somebody who saw Leslie's supper guest enter or leave room 14—in a crowd like that it's almost certain that someone did see him or her, you know, it's only a question of finding the right someone. Besides, the pistol's having been thrown into the Sound was only a guess on my part—not definite enough to use up other people's time."

"I wondered what the dickens you were doing, and why you stayed under water more than on top."

"Simply using my eyes—the bottom's hard sand just there and luckily there's so little wind that the water's clear today. I found it rather farther off shore than I expected."

"What made you guess it was there?"

"Judging the murderer by myself, I felt I'd use the nearest and easiest hiding place—also the action of sand and water would destroy tell-tale fingerprints."

"But how determine its exact location?"

"If you notice, there are shrubs or trees on either side as you look up toward the summer houses, only this one open strip leads straight down to the beach, so I imagined in the darkness the murderer would probably use it in getting close to the water. A medium good throw would be, say, twenty-five feet, so I started quartering the bottom at about that distance out; the pistol was enough to the left of this open space to make me pretty certain it had been thrown by a right-handed person."

"Sounds less difficult, now you've explained. A thirty-two, isn't it?"

"Yes, but of a make I don't know. Aren't those names and markings Italian?" She gave it to him for inspection, watching how his strong fingers handled it with an ease born of long familiarity with firearms.

"Think that odd little inset piece is a trade mark?" He pointed to a small diamond shaped hollow inlaid with red enamel so that its surface lay level with the rest of the pistol stock.

"Looks like the ace of diamonds!" Tam decided after a critical inspection. "And I don't think it's a trade mark; it seems to have been added after the gun was made—just as the owner's initials are sometimes inlaid in a favorite pistol or knife hilt. Sorry to deprive you of it, but my police-trained conscience won't let me leave it even with you, and I must go and dress."

"Oh, see here, I've been looking for you all morning!" he protested. "Surely you aren't heartless enough to instantly disappear again, now that I've found you?"

"I'll be back later on," Tam promised. "I'll even let you offer me a cup of tea after I'm dressed; one gets chilled, staying so long in the water on a cloudy day."

And with that he was forced to rest satisfied, as she ran off in the direction of her cottage boarding place. When Tam reached it she found the Carew maid, Anice, waiting to see her, and with a resigned sigh still further postponed her delayed dressing.

"I've heard you're a detective, Miss," the girl timidly began. "And that you're helping to find out who killed my mistress. Is it true?"

"Yes, Anice. Was there something you thought might help?"

"It's hard to tell, Miss, and I don't like being thought a tale-bearer, only—I'll feel easier if I tell you what happened last night, just after dinner."

"Anything that Mrs. Carew said or did last night may prove important," Tam encouraged. "Don't be afraid to tell me."

"It's about my two ladies, Miss. Of course, being a stranger, you can't guess how the old lady hated young Mrs. Leslie. It was fair awful, Miss, with never a civil word out of her except when Mr. Lord or other people were listening. It's always been like that ever since I came to live with them, before Mr. Eric died; but lately it's got much worse, I don't know why, and last night it came to blows—almost."

"Blows?" Tam echoed the word unbelievingly and the girl hastened to soften her statement.

"Perhaps I shouldn't put it quite so strong, Miss. But when I came up to the dressing room to see if Mrs. Leslie wanted anything before starting, I heard the two of them at it, hammer and tongs. They were in the bed room and the old lady said something, sort of hissing like a snake does; I didn't catch what it was, but Mrs. Leslie cried out, mad as mad: 'You old fiend, I'll teach you not to spread lies!' And she struck her, sharp across the mouth with her open palm. The old lady said never a word, just put a handkerchief to her lips and went out—those big eyes of hers fairly blazing, and— She wasn't in her room till all hours, Miss! I know, because I watched—so I just can't help fearing—"

She evidently dared not put her fears into actual words, but it was not hard to guess that she strongly suspected Mrs. Sarah Carew of having killed her daughter-in-law."

"You did perfectly right to tell me," Tam gravely declared. "And I shan't repeat what you've said unless it becomes absolutely necessary. You have no idea where Mrs. Carew spent the evening?"

"No, Miss. I'm only sure she was out of the house for hours."

"One more question, Anice. Was your mistress perfectly happy in her engagement to Truxton Manning?"

"I think so." But her voice held a hint of doubt. "She seemed very fond of Mr. Manning, but still something's been troubling her just lately; whether it had to do with him or not I can't say. I thought perhaps it was the harm she'd done to other people in the past—kind of troubling her conscience now she was going to be married again and expected to be happy."

"What sort of harm?"

"Not what I could put into plain words, Miss, just the way she'd made Mr. Eric so miserable, and the wildness she'd let have free rein no matter who it hurt."

"By 'wildness' you mean gay parties and perhaps too much drinking?"

"Things of that sort, Miss, yes."

After a few more questions Tam let the girl go and hurried through her own dressing so as not to keep Oakley Calhoun waiting, in spite of which she presently found him before a laden tea table, obviously a prey to keen impatience.

"Heavens, I didn't ask to be invited to dinner!" she declared, eying the dozen or more different kinds of cakes and assorted preserves. "You must have thought I was starving."

"Judged you by myself," he laughed. "I found lunch a stale, insipid meal, probably because I couldn't find you and learn how our case was progressing."

"Since when was it *our* case?" Tam demanded, as she filled his cup. "I thought we were more or less hangers-on to the official inquiry."

"On the contrary." Calhoun smiled at her, his dark eyes crinkling in a delightful way they had. "Wasn't it I who first found the body—that Fitzharris happened to be tagging along is a mere detail, of course—and didn't the coroner particularly ask your assistance?"

"That sounds rather as if you meant constituting your-self my unofficial helper."

"But certainly! I've been pretty well all over the world and mixed up in all sorts of adventures, but I've never yet watched the workings of a murder inquiry from the inside. You don't suppose I intend missing such a chance, do you? Particularly when I came home bent on a long loaf and idleness was already becoming a bore."

"Well," Tam eyed him speculatively. "I don't mind confessing that, while being a woman detective has many advantages, it also carries certain handicaps. Speaking seriously, I think you can be very useful, if your offer is made in earnest."

"It's a bargain, then!" Oakley Calhoun's strong brown hand extended across, the table. "Let's shake on it." Which they accordingly did, then fell to discussing the problem, the solving of which they had jointly agreed to shoulder. Tam told him such of its later developments as she herself knew, while he listened, putting in an occasional shrewd question or comment that showed he was thoroughly interested. They were presently joined by Owen Fitzharris and later Dr. Ramsey appeared in search of Tam.

"One of the State Troopers tells me it was you who found the pistol."

"Yes, I handed it over to them as I came up to the club," Tam explained. "You think it's the one used?"

"Almost certainly. The bullet which I found lodged in Leslie's body is a thirty-two, the same caliber as the pistol you found. I'm in hopes that one of these new-fangled ballistic experts may be able to tell if the bullet surely came from this particular gun."

"Its ownership ought to be easier to trace than that of most weapons," Calhoun volunteered. "Italian makes aren't common in this country."

"That's true, and the odd little red diamond inset should help. We'll concentrate on trying to identify its owner, once we've finished trying to discovering someone who saw Leslie's supper guest."

"There was no other wound or mark on the body?" Tam asked after a little pause, during which all four seemed to be revolving the mysterious murder according to their various lights.

"None at all—" Dr. Ramsey's prompt answer checked itself so abruptly as to leave the impression that he had meant to add something further and suddenly changed his mind. Before Tam could attempt to track down that withheld thought, a bright green roadster dashed up the club drive with a furious haste that ignored such things as speed limits. It halted at the steps, and a woman dressed in almost violent purple fairly flung herself out of the car, approaching the group at the tea table so rapidly that no one had time to rise.

"So you're trying to connect me with Leslie's murder!" She glared at Dr. Ramsey, her eyes aflame with barely controlled rage.

"Now, Rosamond, don't let your temper seize the bit," he soothed. "Sit down and let's talk sensibly."

"Sensibly!" she stormed at him. "Sensibly, when you're searching the countryside for someone who saw me here last night."

"Well, you *were* here, weren't you? And you did quarrel?"

"What if we did? That doesn't say I killed her, though God knows she'd been rotten enough to deserve it—using her leadership here and her reputation for fastidiousness to keep me out of every worth-while house!" She paused for breath, pushing back her mass of dark hair with fingers that trembled from sheer passion. "Of course we quarreled! I came here last night meaning to have it out with her—much satisfaction I got! The little devil refused to abate her attitude one iota! But you've no right to try hunting up evidence to connect me with her death—I can jolly well prove I'd left the club by half past nine. She must have been seen alive after that!"

"As a matter of fact, she wasn't," Ramsey contradicted. "Or at least not by anyone who's so far admitted it."

"Well that's not my fault, and I'll thank you not to drag my name or description into the beastly mess—there's a limit to what I'll stand from you smug hypocrites!" And with that she left them with the same frantic haste as she had appeared, throwing in the clutch of her car with such violence that the outraged gear shrieked protestingly.

"Nice whirlwind of a woman!" Calhoun laughed as he watched the green roadster vanishing down the drive. "I thought she was going literally to attack you, Dr. Ramsey."

"I told you Rosamond always possessed the devil's own temper." He turned to Tam. "Can you see, now, why I don't think it impossible that she killed Leslie in a fit of blind rage?"

"I admit a shade less skepticism; still, we haven't a particle of physical proof against her."

"It may exist nevertheless—I don't intend exempting Rosamond from suspicion until I've satisfied myself that she didn't return to the club grounds after leaving them around nine-thirty."

"Surely she wouldn't rush here to protest against your hunting information against her if she was guilty!" Fitzharris contributed as his opinion.

"Perhaps not—yet on the other hand her coming might be a clever move meant to convey that very impression," Dr. Ramsey retorted, firmly declining to be deprived of his one tangible suspect.

After a little more general talk the group broke up, the two friends again seeing Tam to her boarding place. As they neared it they met the steward, Dorcas Snell, coming from the direction of the village. At sight of Tam she stopped by the roadside, evidently anxious to speak to her, but lacking courage to do so uninvited.

"Did you want to see me, Dorcas?" Tam asked with the natural friendliness which included most of humanity, both saints and sinners.

"Yes, Miss, about something I've remembered Mrs. Carew's asking last night. She wanted to know if the train getting in at 9.28 counted by daylight saving time. I told her no, it meant standard time, because they all do."

"You think she was expecting someone by that train?"

"It's likely, Miss. It would take maybe fifteen minutes to get up here from the station, so if the train was on time, which it generally wasn't, anybody coming by it wouldn't get here much before quarter to ten and they might want to talk a little before starting in to eat. I told you before, she asked if the lettuce would keep crisp until ten."

"As I remember, there are two or three taxis at the station?"

"There are now, Miss. Five years ago my son owned the only one there was, but we've built up considerably since then, so there's business for two or three men in the summer time."

"Suppose I go down to the station," Calhoun offered, "and see if I can pick up anyone who noticed a stranger arriving by the 9.28?"

"We've no reason to feel sure her guest was a stranger to Meadow Dale," Tam pointed out. "And besides, a lot of outside people may have come to the club dance."

"Well, it can't do any harm and one never knows what may turn up in the way of information. If your son's a taxi driver, Dorcas, he may put me in the way of getting to the others."

"Oh, he's dead, sir!" Dorcas sounded rather shocked by his ignorance of the fact. "A matter of two years back. You'll find a nice little freckled man on the taxi stand, sir; he'll help you, I'm sure." And, after something faintly resembling an old-time curtsey, she continued on her way, seemingly quite pleased at having supplied the investigation with one more possibly valuable scrap of information.

"Does a murder inquiry usually limp along with such annoying slowness?" Fitzharris asked discontentedly as they reached Tam's gate. "Here the first day's practically over and as far as I can see nobody's discovered anything."

"Give us time, and please remember that we're up against apparent lack of strong motive and have very few real clues."

"You don't share the coroner's suspicions against Rosamond Forbes?"

"Not yet—what I may think later on it's impossible to predict. At present I'm rather waiting for Truxton Manning's arrival; as Leslie's fiancé I'm hoping he can suggest both a motive and a probable murderer."

5
What Calhoun Found

"It must have been a man who supped with her," Truxton Manning, who had duly arrived by aircraft, asserted. "Otherwise why the secrecy?"

"There's not a single fact to betray the guest's sex either way," Dr. Ramsey quietly informed him.

"I tell you it was a man," Leslie Carew's fiancé reiterated with conviction. "She knew I was due back in a couple of days and she probably had to buy off some old admirer, or pay some damned blackmailer. She knew I wouldn't tolerate the least breath of scandal where she was concerned."

"Why so sure there was a chance of any cropping up?" Tam, whom Dr. Ramsey had asked to be present at his conference with the oil millionaire, inquired.

"What society woman's life is free of that threat? Living in the limelight as they do, someone's always ready to seize on their slightest indiscretion. Don't misunderstand me!" His handsome, rather cruel mouth softened as it had not done throughout the preliminary stages of their conference. "I loved Leslie, and furthermore have no reason to doubt that she deserved every atom of my respect and devotion; still, she was the leader of a gay fashionable set, where the women were not always too virtuous—it's only common sense to realize she may have committed harmless indiscretions that a blackmailer could fasten on, and—she knew one of my main reasons for wanting to marry her was to gain access to a social world I couldn't enter alone, or at least on any better footing than sufferance. To my mind, the absence of that two thousand she's known to have taken to the club with her proves she paid it as hush-money to somebody who knew facts which she didn't want to have reaching my ears."

"So it wasn't altogether a love match?" Tam cut in on a slightly sarcastic note; "The social cloak she could spread over your newly acquired millions played a part."

"What man is averse to such advantages?" Truxton Manning countered. "But my motive for becoming engaged to Leslie hardly affects the present issue; From what you tell me, you're all more or less at sea; no one has a legitimate suspect to offer."

"You're not inclined to take my suspicions of Rosamond Forbes seriously?" Dr. Ramsey asked.

"Not unless, or until, you produce some actual evidence against her. Fact is, I've a suspect of my own who possesses a much stronger motive."

"Blackmail?"

"No."

Truxton Manning fell to a swift pacing up and down the room, as if uncertain as to the wisdom of voicing his suspicions. And Tam, watching him, thought what a splendid specimen of a man he was physically; small wonder that his tall, powerfully knit frame and startlingly handsome face had appealed to the delicate, ultra-refined Leslie Carew. As to his brain, or more literally his nature, she was not so sure. There was something repellant, a hinted understratum of the primitively brutal male—had that quality, also, held its attraction for the polish-surfeited young widow?

"I suppose we'll get nowhere without complete frankness." Manning abruptly ceased his rapid prowling and flung himself into a chair. "As I understand it, Miss O'Brien has your confidence? I may speak openly before her?"

"Surely. She already knows more about the case than I do myself."

"Then I'd better tell you both exactly what I think. You, Dr. Ramsey, as an intimate friend of the family doubtless know how Mrs. Sarah Carew has always hated her daughter-in-law?"

"To be honest, I've never seen any sign of such a feeling on her part," the coroner answered. "Though I have suspected that she was unhappy in their family life."

"Unhappy's a mild way of putting it!" Manning retorted. "She loathed Leslie, always had, even before Eric's death. It seems she considered her as distinctly the wrong wife for her son and has always thought her directly responsible for his suicide. As to the rights of the case, I can't say, naturally having a bias in Leslie's favor; but I do know, both from what she told me and from what I've seen for myself, that since our engagement the former smouldering enmity has burst into hectic flame."

"But why, then, should Leslie's engagement to you anger Sarah Carew?" Ramsey objected. "One might expect her to be glad of anything that took the younger woman out of the house."

"Doubtless she would have been, had Leslie planned leaving it alone; but she meant taking her small son with her. To understand what that meant to Mrs. Carew you must realize that her whole life is centered in the child— to lose him, as she must when Leslie and I returned to my home in California, spelled the end of all things to her. Leslie was very understanding, in talking the matter over with me she showed the utmost generosity of viewpoint, even going so far as to consider asking the child's grandmother to spend several months with us each year so as to be near the boy. It was I who vetoed that plan—and I'm afraid in doing so I brought about Leslie's death!"

"Good God, man! You're not accusing Sarah Carew of having killed her?" Ramsey's voice was filled with horrified incredulity.

"Can you show me anyone with as strong a motive? Don't forget Leslie's removal practically gave Sarah Carew sole charge of her grandson—Mr. Lord being much too easy-going ever to assert his rights against hers. And—the child is the core of her universe."

"It's absurd!" Ramsey hotly protested. "Women don't kill for a reason like that!"

"No?" Manning's, cold blue eyes stared at him with almost arrogant contempt. "Let me tell you I've knocked about the world a good bit and learned in the process that once you scratch a woman's surface conformity to man-made conventions, and get down to bedrock of her love, maternal or sexual, you'll strike the primitive female whose one real passion is to protect and KEEP the thing she loves, regardless of all consequence to those who get in her way! I tell you, under their outward softness women are far less civilized than men!"

"Your experience must have dealt with women of a different class and upbringing than Sarah Carew's," Ramsey insisted. "I can't imagine a thorough-bred of her type ever resorting to violence."

"That comes of having a sheltered imagination," Manning sneered. "Oh, I'll admit all my women haven't been ladies—but I claim neither birth nor training ever destroys the potential tigress chained in every woman's nature. What say, Miss O'Brien?"

His piercing eyes suddenly demanded her truth in response to his, from the slender girl so quietly listening.

"Probably Dr. Ramsey won't forgive me, but I can't avoid favoring your suspect above his." She discreetly refrained from argument as to the truth of his more general thesis; after all, it had nothing to do with the immediate business in hand, and was only interesting because of the side-light it threw on Manning's own character. "He may be more inclined to agree with us when he's heard certain facts told me by Leslie's maid."

She repeated Anice's story of the after-dinner quarrel ending in a blow, then added her further assertion that Sarah Carew had been absent from the house during the critical hours proceeding, and directly following, Leslie's murder.

"Phew!" Manning allowed himself a long self-congratulatory whistle. "Still think I'm barking up the wrong tree, Dr. Ramsey?"

"It would take considerably more than a feminine quarrel and a few hours unaccounted for, to convince me of Sarah Carew's guilt," The coroner responded stiffly.

"Even with a blow thrown in? Or can't that sluggish imagination of yours visualize what that meant to a proud, sensitive woman, already on the rack because of threatened separation from her grandchild?"

Ramsey only shook a stubborn negtive, refusing to accept the possibility of Mrs. Carew's guilt.

"Oh well, if you won't, you won't." The big millionaire shrugged resignedly. "Looks to me, Miss O'Brien, as if it was up to us to prove my theory right or wrong! Are you willing to come in on my side?"

"Not possible," she told him with calm finality. "To take sides at all would end my usefulness. Open eyes and mind are a detective's first necessity; surely you see that."

"Meaning that only the truth concerns you, and you'll hang on its trail regardless of where it leads. All the same, I haven't seen you trotting out any hopeful suspects!"

"First of all I want to know more about Leslie's supper guest. Have the fingerprint reports come in yet, Dr. Ramsey?"

"Oh, yes, but they tell us almost nothing. As you know, the action of sand and water thoroughly freed the pistol of any fingerprints it may have borne; and as for the other articles, wine glass, candles, and the rest, whoever handled them either wiped off tell-tall marks or used gloves."

"It's important to know which," Tam declared. "The former might have been done by anyone with a working knowledge of crook methods—but the latter spells premeditation."

"I suppose you're right," he conceded, "though it hadn't struck me in quite that light. Tomorrow I'll get in touch with the man who sent in the report and ask if he can settle that point."

"Please do, and you haven't yet told us his report on Room 14."

"Why—" The tired coroner looked more than a little guilty. "While the State Trooper and I went over the room, it didn't occur to me to connect it with the murder closely enough to make taking photographs of any prints there necessary!"

"Oh, Lord!" Tam's clever young face frankly confessed her disgust. "So I suppose the room's been straightened by now, and all the silver and china carefully washed!"

"It's of no consequence," Manning suddenly cut in. "You'll find that supper had nothing to do with the murder—they're two distinct episodes."

"Why so certain?"

"Call it a hunch, if you like; I, for one, am banking on it. Take my advice, Miss O'Brien, let the side issues alone and concentrate on Sarah Carew." Truxton Manning rose with the ease of a man who has spent much of his life out of doors. "It's too late for decisive action tonight, so we'll postpone further plan of battle till tomorrow. I'm staying at Dune House; may I give you a lift home, Miss O'Brien?"

"Thanks, no. I want a few minutes with Dr. Ramsey."

"My exit cue." A quizzical edge to his smile made her suspect him of guessing the object of those few desired minutes. "Goodnight; I'll see you both in the morning."

When he had gone, Tam turned to Dr. Ramsey with a question:

"At what time should you say Leslie Carew died?"

"In the close neighborhood of eleven o'clock," he told her without the slightest hesitation, sure enough of his ground once it touched on his beloved profession. "She was found a few minutes after one—I'm judging by the condition of her body when I first saw and touched it, and by the stage of digestion reached, as shown by the autopsy."

"Then it was she who ate the supper salad?"

"On the contrary, she had eaten nothing at all since her eight o'clock dinner. It was to that meal I referred."

So Tam had been right in attributing the healthy appetite as evinced by the remnants of the supper, to guest rather than hostess.

"So you feel pretty certain she was killed at, or near, eleven," Tam thoughtfully repeated. "Do you happen to know at what time this morning Truxton Manning's lawyer located him in Chicago?"

"I'm afraid I don't follow." The doctor sounded a trifle dazed.

"Simply a question of time between the two points. If nothing was heard from him before, say, seven or eight this morning, it's just possible that he might have left here after Leslie's death and still reached Chicago by a fast plane in time to send Mr. Lord that wire."

"My God! You're not suspecting *him* of shooting her?"

"Suspect's much too strong a word—I only wondered. Suppose we have someone in Chicago find out if he was really there last night."

"Just as you like, though it seems to me we'll end by suspecting every reputable citizen of Meadow Dale."

"With so little to go on, we can't afford leaving any loose ends lying about." She smiled encouragingly. "You'll feel more cheerful after a good night's sleep—and remember that, after all, the inquiry's less than twenty-four hours old." With which consoling thought she left him, refusing his offer to drive her home. "It's not really late and the night's so beautiful I shall enjoy the walk."

Which, in fact, she did, being one of those genuine country lovers who find most satisfaction in solitary enjoyment of rural beauty. Her cottage boarding place was in darkness, save for a single dim light left burning for her, and instead of entering she sat down on the honeysuckle-draped steps, tempted by the warm moon-washed night into further lingering out of doors.

Unlike most detectives, Tam seldom made written notes on a case or compiled lists of unanswered questions. She believed that the more one trusted one's memory the more it justified such confidence. So now she lighted that most soothing of counsellors, a cigarette, and began chronologically rehearsing the developments of the past twenty-four hours.

Up to the moment, only two tangible suspects had turned up, both of them women, and at the present stage of the inquiry Tam found herself unable to seriously believe in the guilt of either one. Of the strong driving power of Rosamonds' supposed motive she entertained decided doubts, while her rejection of Sarah Carew as a convincing suspect was mainly due to the strange accessories amongst which Leslie's body had been found; no matter how desperately the older woman might have hated her, Tam felt that she would never have thus exposed the dead mother of her idolized grandson.

In the final analysis, did not the key to the whole problem lie in the puzzling details of that same stage-set? The playing cards, the empty wine glass, the sprinkled sugar—what meaning lay behind them all? And what conceivable significance had that white oblong of wrapping paper with its printed numbers: "997033?"

Here Tam sighed impatiently, crushed out her cigarette and lighted a second. As she did so the insistent call of a whip-poor-will came from just outside the cottage gate. It was unobtrusive, perfectly done, yet she realized the hour was all wrong; it was much too late for the cry of any self-respecting evening bird. Tam rose and took an uncertain step or two down the little path, then advanced with more decision as a tall, lounging shadow separated itself from the surrounding trees and stood close beside the gate; surely it was Oakley Calhoun.

"I saw the flare of your match and guessed it must be you," he apologized as she joined him. "So I couldn't resist bidding for a few minutes chat."

"And what are you doing, roaming this part of the countryside so late? Unless I'm mistaken, Owen Fitzharris' cottage is on the other side of the club."

"If you *will* insist on asking embarrassing questions, I've been making acquaintances with the village speak-easy."

"Really? I'd no idea it possessed such a thing."

"Neither had I, but the freckle-faced taxi driver of whom Dorcas told us introduced me. It's quite a flourishing concern, give you my word."

"Must carry rather decent stuff," came Tam's critical comment. "You don't look any the worse."

"Oh, I follow the precepts of the Buddha, practicing moderation in all things." He laughed. "But aren't you interested in the result of my strenuous labors on your behalf?"

"Mine?"

"Certainly. Didn't I volunteer to track down any strangers arriving on last night's 9:28?"

"You haven't been at it all this time?"

"More or less," he acknowledged. "Dorcas' freckled-faced friend was easy enough to find, but one of the other taxi drivers who frequent the station proved as elusive as a hot-weather flea—he was supposed to be back at the stand by sundown, instead of which he never turned up at all. Freckle-Face and I've been trailing him hither and thither until we finally ran him to earth in said speak-easy. Of course he was the only one of the village drivers who had anything to tell."

"Why of course?"

"General contrariness of life; aren't the people who have, or know, something we want, always the hardest to discover? Still it wasn't altogether wasted effort. This chap, name of Jones, by the bye, says a veiled and cloaked woman got off the 9:28 last night, scurried into his taxi which happened to be the nearest, snapping out just three words: 'The country club!' She didn't speak again until they were just inside the club gates, then told him to stop, paid him and got out disappearing among the trees that grow thick on the water side of the drive—the side where the summer house stands."

"Good work!" Tam applauded. "It gives us our first real hint about Leslie's supper guest—for I suppose it must have been she; no woman would wear a veil on a hot summer night unless she was bent on preserving the utmost secrecy. I suppose he couldn't furnish any definite description?"

"Pretty vague," Calhoun cheerfully admitted. "I fancy he'd visited the speak-easy before that train arrived and was none too clear visioned—but he thinks the woman was tall, and he's certain she moved more swiftly than anybody

he'd ever seen before; indeed the rapidity of all her mo-
tions seems the thing about her that most impressed him."

"Dark or fair?"

"He couldn't say; doesn't seem to have really looked."

"You've helped wonderfully—" She began, then stopped
at sight of his delighted grin.

"Save your thanks until I've passed on the crowning
item!" he begged. "I've saved it till last, just as kids save
their choice bit of candy."

"There's more?"

"Um-hum— When the veiled lady hopped out with her
customary speed, she dropped something. Jones heard it
fall but didn't realize its nature until he'd started to turn
the car and his headlights picked out a vicious looking
little pistol—then he shouted after his vanished passenger,
who suddenly reappeared, snatched up the gun and vanished again. Whether she'd heard his call or simply missed
the weapon and come back for it, Jones wasn't sure."

"The pistol!" Tam felt strongly tempted to hug him.
"That's the first gleam we've caught as to its ownership!
Evidently, Mr. Calhoun, I was playing what Truxton Manning would call a 'true hunch' when I decided to annex
you."

6
Thirty Thousand Dollars

The inquest, held the following afternoon at Dune House, brought to light no new evidence and simply resulted in the timeworn verdict: "Willful murder by person or persons unknown."

When it was over Mr. Lord, the slain woman's father, asked the Coroner, Ramsey, Tam, and Oakley Calhoun, who was beginning to be recognized as her informal coadjutor, to remain behind the rest for a consultation. Tam had that morning told Dr. Ramsey of the taxi-driver's mysterious fare, but both he and Mr. Lord now wanted Oakley Calhoun's own account of what had been learned. They were still speculating as to the veiled lady's identity when a small, very much out of breath boy dashed up to the side porch where they were sitting, loudly calling for Dr. Ramsey.

"It's Ma—she's took awful bad!" he panted. "Don't guess she'll live unless you come quick!"

Dr. Ramsey, who seemed to know the youngster, stopped for no questions but rushed into the house in quest of his medical bag. A moment later they heard his car chugging wildly down the drive.

"I'd place him as a better physician than coroner," Calhoun hazarded. Mr. Lord nodded tolerantly.

"His heart's in his healing of the sick—such doctors are born, never made."

There was a little pause which Calhoun broke with a question. "Struck me he was withholding some finding of his autopsy—either of you get the same idea?"

"I did," Tam instantly responded. "In fact it's not the first time I've suspected him of keeping something back." Then, her quick eye catching an approaching figure, she added: "You're about to have a visitor, Mr. Lord; let's hope he's not a reporter."

Following the direction of her gaze the others saw a slight, rather undersized man arrayed in a suit of violent summer check, who rapidly approached from the side of the grounds bordering the dunes which gave the house its name. His manner showed no trace of uncertainty or embarrassment, as, reaching the low steps, he mounted them, removing his panama with an impressive flourish.

"Howdy, everybody—trust I don't intrude."

"You—you—" Mr. Lord stuttered, his voice actually trembling with rage. "How dare you show your face here?"

"Gently, gently—excitement's bad for the aged, particularly on a hot day." The visitor flopped into a convenient chair where he sat fanning a face that still retained traces of great personal beauty, now gone thoroughly to seed.

"Shall I throw him off the place, sir?" Calhoun hopefully inquired, whereat the stranger favored him with a vicious scowl, before turning back to Mr. Lord.

"Quite some time since we've met, eh, Father-in-Law? Odd how a death in the family draws its members together."

"Better let me remove him." Calhoun straightened from his lounging position against the rail and eyed Mr. Lord inquiringly.

"Not yet; I must know what's given him courage to venture here; besides the swine's not fit to soil a gentleman's hands."

"Swine! Tut tut, Father-in-Law—is that a proper way to describe your beloved daughter Lydia's husband?" He laughed again, but the brilliant, dissipated eyes were venomous.

"Answer—why are you here?" Mr. Lord demanded.

"Only the little matter of Leslie's will. The papers state she died intestate, which I happen to know is a lie."

"It's a fact," Mr. Lord retorted. "Leslie never made a will, and by the terms of her husband's everything goes to the child."

"Not everything! Lydia, my wife, inherits a cool thirty thousand, and she gets it too—" he added in a sudden snarl, "or I'll make it hot for you and the brat."

"Thirty thousand!" Mr. Lord echoed on a note of scorn. "You're insane, or else trying to carry through a colossal bluff."

"Insane, am I? Just you look in Leslie's jewel safe and you'll find proof of what I say! I tell you she made a will not three weeks ago—in it Lydia's named to get thirty thousand."

"Rubbish! You've fleeced this family out of every cent you'll ever get—now go, before I call a servant to run you off the place."

For an instant the visitor hesitated, then rose with a nonchalant slowness. "Oh, I'll go; no inducement, wet or otherwise, to stick round this morgue. Only, see that you hunt up Leslie's will. These two—" with a wave of his hand that included both Tam and Calhoun, "will have to back me up under oath that I told you where to find it. Ta-ta, Daddy-in-Law!"

And with that he departed, aggressively swaggering, while Mr. Lord stared after him, eyes blood-shot with helpless fury. As the talkative check suit disappeared in the distance he turned to his guests with a gesture of apology.

"Sorry to have inflicted a family scene on comparative strangers—Chadwick probably preferred making his absurd claim before witnesses, though what he hoped to gain rather puzzles me."

"Please don't attribute the question to idle curiosity—but is he really your son-in-law?"

"Yes, Miss O'Brien, I grieve to say he is."

"I don't quite understand; I thought Leslie's husband was dead."

"And so he is. Has no one told you that I—once—had another daughter, Lydia?"

"No. I thought Leslie an only child."

"She was the youngest, but not the only one. Probably Lydia dropped from sight so long ago that people have ceased mentioning her unless she is especially recalled to their minds."

He seemed to contemplate no further explanation. But Tam, with the memory of certain letters scratched on a supper-cloth, had no intention of letting the matter drop. "L. C." might stand for "Lydia Chadwick" equally well as for "Leslie Carew!"

"Mr. Lord!" Her beautiful Irish voice was intensely serious. "To a detective, every fact concerning the murder-victim is important. I should have been informed that Leslie possessed a sister."

"Surely the fact has nothing to do with her death!" he remonstrated. "Lydia's unfortunate marriage occurred nearly ten years ago; since which time the sisters have not met. I forebade it."

"Which doesn't in the least prove that they may not have kept up some sort of communication without your knowledge," Tam retorted. "The fact that Lydia's husband claims to know of a recently-made will may indicate secrets in Leslie's life of which you have no inkling. I'm afraid

I must beg that you either tell me your older daughter's story, or send me to some reliable person who can give me its main features."

"I quite fail to see the necessity—" Mr. Lord complained. "Still, if you insist—"

"I must."

"There is really very little to tell. Lydia, unlike her younger sister, never cared at all for fashionable society— by nature she was adventurous, not to say reckless, and loved excitement above all things. Her unfortunate meeting with Miles Chadwick occurred during a visit to New Orleans, in which city he was, so I afterwards learned, a professional gambler and race track man. At that time he was, even I must admit it, a remarkably handsome man, and he had acquired a certain superficial polish which deceived Lydia's eyes. She fell violently in love with him and, despite my utmost efforts to prevent the catastrophe, ended by eloping. After their marriage I attempted to condone it and tolerate Chadwick; but he was impossible, an utter cad. After only a few weeks it ended in my forbidding him the house—Lydia espousing his cause and going with him. Later, rumors reached me that things went from bad to worse. Chadwick squandered all his wife's private fortune and—but the remainder is almost too shameful to repeat."

"In the interest of the investigation, I had better hear it." Tam quietly insisted.

"Three years ago, a member of the Government Narcotic squad came to me seeking information as to the whereabouts of my eldest daughter and her husband. When I had convinced the man that I hadn't heard from either of them in years, he told me how Chadwick had entered the drug trade and was then wanted on a charge of having smuggled into the country, and distributed, quantities of illicit drugs a charge which, to my unspeakable horror, included Lydia, who was accused of having aided and abetted him!"

"Then, in perfectly plain language, both Miles Chadwick and his wife—your daughter—are wanted by the narcotic agents?"

"I suppose that is an accurate statement of the facts." Mr. Lord sorrowfully acknowledged.

"Is it still true that you've no idea where your daughter is?"

"I have neither seen nor heard from her since she left my house nearly ten years ago."

"If you for any reason wanted to find her, how would you go about it?"

"Really I should be utterly at a loss—perhaps I might advertise."

"Surely you at least remember who were formerly her closest friends?"

"Only very hazily. A busy man doesn't particularly notice all the young people who over-run his home. In fact, I think Rosamond Forbes is the only one I remember distinctly, and probably that exception is due to her having remained more or less constantly in the picture ever since."

"Nice idea of the ludicrous our youngsters are developing!" Dr. Ramsey suddenly popped out of the French window, mopping a heated and indignant brow, "That little imp's mother wasn't in the least sick—he only meant to be funny!"

"Deserves a good thrashing," Mr. Lord absently sympathized. "Who do you suppose turned up just now, but Miles Chadwick."

For a second or two the name seemed to touch no responsive cord in Ramsey's brain, then its significance penetrated. "Lydia's husband! Lord, what a nerve!"

His host repeated Chadwick's story of a recently made will; whereupon the coroner, his sense of duty touched, instantly proposed that they look into Leslie's jewel safe, on the off chance that Chadwick might have been telling the truth. All four, under their host's reluctant guidance, repaired to Leslie's luxurious dressing room, where Anice gave them the jewel safe's combination.

Greatly to Mr. Lord's astonishment, the will was actually there, and furthermore, examination proved that Chadwick's claim of thirty thousand dollars having been left to his wife was based on literal fact.

That question settled, Tam and Calhoun left Dr. Ramsey to console their disgruntled host.

"What's your next move?" Calhoun presently asked, watching her intent expression with a faintly quizzical smile.

"Intend finding Lydia Chadwick, if it's humanly possible." Tam emerged from an absorbed reverie. "She's a new pawn in the game, or at least one we've only just heard of, and she sounds well worth investigating."

"You think *she* was Leslie's supper guest?"

"Don't you?"

He nodded. "If she was, the guest's having drawn Leslie's initials instead of her own ceases to be a puzzle—she didn't, they simply happen to own the same ones. Also the fact that Lydia's wanted by the police would explain the singular secrecy."

"Not the police—the narcotic squad," she corrected.

"Same thing, or almost. Was I wrong in thinking you fished for the names of Lydia's friends with the idea of tracing her through them?"

"Only got Rosamond Forbes," Tam lamented, "and she strikes me as an anything but promising subject—besides, she knows I'm a detective and will be very much on guard.

Awful person, that Chadwick, wasn't he? Of course it was he who arranged to have Dr. Ramsey called away, so he couldn't ask embarrassing questions in his official capacity as coroner."

Calhoun chuckled. "Fooled the poor man completely, too. He's no suspicion the boy was put up to pulling his practical joke."

"He wouldn't! They're both dears, he and Mr. Lord, but in a murder investigation they're about as useful as two well-meaning tabbies. This whole inquiry's been filled with mistakes—for instance, the cleaning of room 14 before a fingerprint expert had gone over it, was simply inexcusable. And the worst of it is I've gone far enough into the case to feel personally responsible."

"Because Dr. Ramsey asked your assistance, or because the mystery itself has gripped you?"

"A little of both, perhaps, but much more because I've been taught all my life that those trained to run down evil-doers owe a duty to society that they can't evade. They've no right to sit back and let a criminal escape detection simply because they're not officially engaged to catch him. Probably it's something like the obligation to heal bodily ills felt by a physician. In an emergency he could never turn from a person needing medical help, and it's the same with us—we must spend our acquired skill in the struggle to eliminate mental ills. I'd feel I was aiding and abetting Leslie Carew's murderer if I stepped out and left the coroner to muddle along alone. Judging by what you've already seen, don't you think that if the mystery surrounding her death is ever to be cleared away, it's up to us to do it?"

"I fear me you're right, though I doubt if you're wise to depend much on my assistance. I'll admit feeling considerably more fogged now than I did in the beginning."

"That's because you're unaccustomed to the habit different trails have, of turning back on themselves, crossing each other, and generally getting snarled into a hopeless tangle. Later on they'll begin separating and straightening out. Meanwhile I'm going to get my car from the village garage and drive out to the Willows."

"Am I allowed to tag along?"

"Not this time. It's easier to manage a woman without masculine onlookers, and I suspect Rosamond's going to prove difficult.—By the way, I wonder what's become of Truxton Manning? He disappeared the instant the inquest was over."

"So I noticed." A dry note in Oakley Calhoun's pleasantly lazy voice, made her glance at him; only his unrevealing profile was to be seen as he lounged easily along beside her, his long stride fitting itself to her shorter feminine steps.

"Why that tone?"

"No special reason—only wondered if you'd caught what bit of evidence it was that so upset the oil man."

"Never even noticed that he was upset. Please tell me about it."

"I've cudgeled my brains trying to remember exactly what stage the inquest had reached, when I last saw him looking normally interested—it can't be done. All I know is, that toward the end he looked like a sheep being led to the slaughter. You'd imagine the verdict was brought in against him!"

"Pity we don't know what bothered him! We went pretty thoroughly over the case last night, and none of the evidence seemed to disturb him. Now, what fresh facts came out today?"

She lapsed into intent thought, neither speaking again until the village was almost reached, then Tam administered a mental shake and flung him a smile.

"Don't mind if I sometimes forget you're here; it's only the working of what a friend of my father calls the 'Bloodhound instinct.'"

"I know." He nodded understandingly. "Thrill-of-the-chase sort of thing. Do you overtake anything that throws a light on Truxton Manning's upset?"

"Not a glimmer, and the worst of it is I feel knowing would prove a decided help. Well, here's the garage; if you care to stop by, after supper, I'll let you know what Rosamond Forbes says, or more probably, doesn't say."

7
The Fifty-Three Club

On reaching The Willows, a smaller estate than Dune House but equally lovely, Tam learned that Mrs. Forbes was somewhere in the gardens.

"I think I can find her, Miss, if you'll wait a few minutes." The maid obligingly offered.

"Don't trouble, I'll hunt her up myself," Tam answered, strongly suspecting that Rosamond might evade seeing her unless taken by surprise.

The gardens proved more extensive than they looked from the house and for some time she could see no sign of their mistress. Then, rounding the corner of an ornamental hedge, she caught sight of two figures in the middle distance. The man's powerful shoulders and unusual height made her certain he was Truxton Manning. And—she could almost have sworn that something passed from his hand to the woman's, in the instant before they saw her coming.

If she was right, whatever had so changed hands was skillfully hidden before Tam neared them.

"Why, Miss O'Brien, how nice of you to look me up!" There was not a trace in Rosamond's voice or manner of yesterday's stormy wrath. "Truxton's just been telling me how he's pinning all his hopes on your being able to solve

our terrible enigma. He says Dr. Ramsey has no more idea
than a rabbit, of how to conduct a murder inquiry."

"See here, Rosamond, that remark was strictly private—not meant for publication." Maiming expostulated
with just a hint of real anger under his laughing tone.
"Though if Miss O'Brien is altogether honest, I'll bet she
agrees with the sentiment expressed."

"Professional ethics forbid. I'm supposed to be assisting Dr. Ramsey."

"Assisting's good; more likely, you're doing the major
part of the work. Any new developments?"

Because of what Calhoun had said, she was intently
studying him, and believed that she had caught a note
of anxious dread in the voice he strove to keep perfectly
normal.

"Nothing to speak of," she answered. "Only, a point
has come up on which we hope Mrs. Forbes can help us."

"Of course I'll be delighted! Do run along, Truxton,
that's a dear. Miss O'Brien and I want to talk."

"Why can't I play silent listener?" He appeared curious
as to the point of which Tam had spoken.

"Hard as you may find it to believe you'd be *de trop,*"
Rosamond assured him. "Men always are when two women
want to speak frankly. Don't be stubborn, you're wasting
Miss O'Brien's precious time."

The oil man could hardly linger in the face of such urgent
dismissal, so grumblingly departed, leaving them alone.

"Now do tell me instantly how I can help."

Tam had revolved various methods of extracting the
desired information, deciding that if she could make
Rosamond believe it was to Lydia's advantage to be found,
she would be most likely to help; and after all the contents
of Leslie's will was bound to become public property within the next few days—Lydia's absence would only forestall
its probating.

"We've found that Leslie Carew left her sister a fairly large sum of money, and we've no possible way of notifying her of the legacy. Mr. Lord thought you might possibly know where Lydia is."

"Now, I wonder why he thought that?" Rosamond sounded genuinely puzzled.

"He says you used to be Lydia's closest friend."

"That's true, but I haven't seen her in ages, not for more years than I like to count."

"So you can't help us at all?"

"So frightfully sorry, my dear, but I'm absolutely helpless—I haven't the faintest idea how to go about finding her."

"You don't even know any other friend, who may have kept in touch with her?" Tam persisted.

"Not one. All our old crowd has scattered; I barely remember their names. After all this time."

"There's another way you could help—by giving us one of Lydia's old pictures, if you happen to have saved one."

"I'm afraid I haven't any," Rosamond began, then abruptly checked herself. "It's just possible that I can find one for you. Let's go up to the house, and if you're not in a hurry, I'll search through an old box I have, filled with treasured keepsakes of my girlhood."

The suggested search proved a rather long one. Tam waited almost an hour before her hostess reappeared, beaming triumphantly.

"It's old and rather faded, but quite good of Lydia at that time," she announced, handing Tam a cabinet-sized photograph of a laughing girl dressed in the fashion of a decade ago.

Tam carried it to the window, studying features and expression with intent so to impress the face on her mind that she would know it in any crowd, providing it had not in the meantime changed past recognition.

"She doesn't seem to have in the least resembled her sister—Leslie's features were much more delicately cut; even the coloring's different."

"It wasn't very different, really," Rosamond quickly protested. "That picture's rather deceiving about the coloring; it makes Lydia too dark. And of course she's changed a lot since then."

She bit the last word short, glancing guiltily at Tam to see if she had noticed the slip. Then, reassured by her visitor's look of tranquil unconsciousness, Rosamond hurried on to express fervent hopes for the success of their search for the missing Lydia.

"Thanks so much for the picture—and if you think of any way we might trace her, I'm sure you'll let me know."

They separated with cordial farewells and Tam, reentering her car, started back to the village. So Rosamond had lied! She reflected over the incident, curious as to what motive lay behind her denial of all present knowledge as to Lydia's whereabouts. If Rosamond had really not seen her for so many years, why the certainty that Lydia had altered so much since the photograph was taken? Rather a stupid slip, Tam considered it, and one which a cleverer woman could have covered or at least ameliorated, instead of simply looking guilty.

And why was Truxton Manning so evidently upset, so loath to leave her alone with Rosamond? Was there something the oil millionaire feared she might tell, and if so, whom did it concern? Surely the only woman whose secrets might be expected to deeply interest him was his fiancée—already dead and past hurting by their exposure.

That evening Oakley Calhoun found her an absent-minded, not to say snappy companion. He finally took her to task with an accusation of refusing to share her worries when by so doing she might save him from encroachment of his oldest and most deadly enemy, ennui.

"It's not exactly worry," she smiled at him with a friendliness capable, so he considered, of atoning for much worse slights than any of mere inattention. "I'm only trying to decide on the next move. So far, we've done nothing but

follow blind alleys that led nowhere, and even now I can't determine who, among the various people concerned, really possesses a key capable of unlocking the mystery of Leslie's murder."

"Quite sure the key lies here in Meadow Dale?"

"Not a bit sure," she ruefully confessed, "and I am beginning to glimpse more sinister possibilities than at first. Remember what Mr. Lord said about Chadwick and his wife's being wanted for drug traffic?"

"Surely."

"Do you think that granulated sugar scattered under Leslie's body could, in the murderer's mind, have represented morphine?"

"It's a fantastic thought—but you've believed all along that every item of the murder scene held a meaning; perhaps you've hit on one. Does it lead anywhere in particular?"

"Not at the moment—only opens wider possibilities. Do you know," she crunched out her cigarette and leaned toward him. "I've a feeling Rosamond is the one most likely to repay watching. She seems our only hope of finding Lydia Chadwick—for I'm certain she lied about having lost touch with her."

"And you very much want to get hold of the fair Lydia?"

"Naturally! We think she was Leslie's mysterious guest and probably the last person to see her alive—with the exception of the murderer—which part, by the way, the thirty thousand left by her sister's will gives Lydia a certain motive for assuming."

"Seriously meaning—"

"No more than that Lydia's a possibility we can't afford overlooking. In a murder case, even the nearest relations aren't exempt from suspicion, you know. Oh, dear! If someone opened up my brain and looked inside, they'd find nothing but a flock of question marks! Do let's talk about something else—books, the Orient, anything but crimes and criminals."

The following day Leslie Carew's lovely body was duly consigned to its final resting place, and after the funeral Dr. Ramsey took Tam aside to tell her that a member of the State Police had unearthed a filling station man who claimed to have fixed a flat tire for Rosamond Forbes, soon after twelve o'clock on the night of the club dance.

"Of course I've questioned her about it," he finished. "But, she insists the filling station owner is simply mistaken in the night—says she drove directly home after leaving the club about nine thirty, and didn't leave the house again that night."

In the face of this new bit of evidence Tam felt justified in arranging to have an unobtrusive watch kept on Rosamond's movements, by the State Police. The first time they got wind of any planned trip into New York City, Tam was to be instantly notified.

She reasoned that if Rosamond and Lydia were still friends, as she more than half believed, the former might feel the need of warning Lydia that she was being sought, and in that way lead Tam to the desired lady. It was two days before anything of the sort showed symptoms of happening; then she got word that Mrs. Forbes had ordered her big car for an evening trip to the city. Tam laid her plans accordingly. When the Forbes limousine swept out of the village and headed for New York, Tam's roadster trailed along at a discreet distance.

"Probably she's going on some perfectly innocent visit and we'll have our trouble for our pains," she pessimistically remarked to Calhoun as they cleared the last houses and gained open country. "At best, our learning anything is only the chanciest sort of a gamble."

"What else is life?" he retorted, with the light-hearted laugh of one to whom long chances are as the breath of open spaces.

It turned out an unexciting chase; traffic and signal lights favored them so that they were only once in any real danger of losing Rosamond's car; then a heavy truck crowded between, slowed, and lost them the last of a green light. Their quarry gained several blocks, while the stop light held them inactive. Luck again favored, however, and after a little they picked up the limousine and thereafter stuck close to its tail light.

The city was crossed and Rosamond's car headed down a quiet side street on the upper West Side. It was then Calhoun's watchfulness saved them from failure; for while the limousine waited near the curb for a change of lights Rosamond slipped quietly out of her car and turned back, on foot, the way they had come—only Calhoun's touch on Tam's arm made her catch the maneuver, as her eyes had been fixed on the signal light.

The limousine went on, minus its passenger, and they lost precious minutes in parking the roadster and dashing back on foot. For a little Tam thought they had lost her; then she recognized Rosamond's tall figure at the door of a house halfway down the block, and, as she seemed to be bestowing not the slightest attention on passers-by, they risked a closer approach.

The house was in absolute darkness, not a glimmer of light anywhere, but that fact in no wise discouraged Rosamond; she first knocked on the door's wooden panel, then pressed a bell at one side, ending by another series of knocks. There was a moment's delay, then a small bright light hidden in the carved woodwork above the door flashed on, so illuminating Rosamond that anyone looking out through a concealed peep-hole could easily distinguish face and figure. It burned only a second or two then the door opened on complete darkness and Rosamond slipped inside.

"Shall we try to bluff our way in?" Calhoun asked as they both took mental note of the house number, neither writing it down.

"No. We'd fail to a moral certainty, besides advertising that we're after Rosamond. Much better work it another way."

She glanced at her wrist watch, noted that the hour was still early, then headed for the nearest drugstore that might be reasonably expected to boast a telephone. He waited while she made a brief call, then both returned to the roadster.

"We're headed for police headquarters," she informed him, settling for the downtown run. "Not meaning to stage a raid, or anything of that sort—only to ask help from one of my old friends there. I just had him on the wire and he'll wait for us."

"Suppose that house is one of the night clubs Prohibition has made spring up all over the lot," Calhoun hazarded. "Gloomy enough from outside, not a crack of light shown."

"Tight fitting inner shutters—they're fairly common."

"Lot of red tape needed to get in, and they're cautious about the signal; Rosamond's first knock was two short and three long, the ring two, a pause, then two more; and the second knock just reversed the first. Not a series likely to be hit on by accident."

"You've sharp eyes."

"Have to have, where I've lived most—otherwise a fellow wouldn't live!"

Inspector Peter McCoy, whose friendship for Tam dated from her cradle days, warmly welcomed her, but eyed her companion a trifle askance. The Inspector was unused to seeing her closely associated with anyone of so obviously different a world than his own; and this tall, detached-looking stranger, who wore his clothes with something approaching the careless ease of a well-bred Englishman, was markedly different from the average American. Where the deuce had she collected him, and why? His glance inquired.

"Suppose you want to bother this overworked force for some facts or other," McCoy grumbled, when his hopeful waiting for some explanation of the stranger had lengthened until it threatened to become an awkward pause.

Tam, who had pretty accurately gauged his thought and harbored not the slightest intention of gratifying his curiosity, grinned cheerfully.

"Of course. Carrying my cases through to the finish would cost triple what it does now, if I hadn't the police to fall back on for information I haven't time to hunt up for myself. This time it's a night club on the upper West Side." She gave him street and number. "Know anything about it?"

"The Homicide Bureau takes no interest in night clubs unless they produce a corpse or two," McCoy retorted. "If Conway Fisk is still in the building, he's your man. Since his promotion he's been specially detailed to keep an eye on those mushrooms—they spring up and wither so fast, they need constant watching."

After a little delay, Lieutenant Fisk was found by one of McCoy's men, and, hearing who wanted details of a certain night club, agreed to come to the Inspector's office and supply them.

"It's about the oldest club of its kind in the city," he explained. "The man who runs it is either remarkably intelligent or he's got psychic powers; there's never any liquor in sight when any of us drift in, no matter how carefully we're got up for the part of innocent patron. I've heard that the place was started as a semi-private dancing club and was supposed never to enroll more than fifty-two members, each one to be officially known by a designated card from a playing deck instead of by name. Since then, it's grown in popularity and members, way past the original plan; but there are still only the limited number of full members, the places of the charter members who dropped out having been refilled from a waiting list—all the others who frequent the place are known as guests and haven't the full privileges of the regular crew. So far the club's been run on exclusive lines, catering only to carefully selected people, and has never got into serious trouble. Only wish a few more of them would follow the example of this Fifty-Three Limited!"

"Why Fifty-Three?" Tam inquired. "I thought you said the membership was confined to the number in an ordinary playing deck."

"Oh, they include the Joker—a card that's said to belong to Davis, the proprietor."

"Are you on good enough terms with him to get us in there tonight?"

Fisk considered. He knew Tam well enough to feel certain she wanted admission to the club because some trail she was following led within its doors.

"I'd have to guarantee you'd make no arrest, and no report to headquarters," he finally decided.

"Surely," Tam agreed. "You can even say we're out-of-town friends who want a glimpse of New York night life. We'll promise to do nothing that might undeceive him."

"Then I think it can be arranged." Nor was he mistaken. When the supposed situation was explained over the phone to the night club proprietor, he was at first suspicious, but on receiving Lieutenant Fisk's positive guarantee of non-interference, decided it might not be a bad idea to strengthen friendly relations by acceding to the unusual request. If the Lieutenant's friends would present a Joker with Fisk's last name written across it, he promised them admission.

As they drove back uptown, Calhoun was aware that his thoughts insisted on straying from their immediate adventure to the girl who shared it with him. A dozen questions hovered on his tongue tip, all of which he resolved to put at the first opportunity; for while personal questions might not be in the best of taste, a woman who never talked about herself was such an anomaly that she deserved different treatment from the rest of her sex. Also, once his burning curiosity was slaked, thoughts of this fascinating, self-possessed young person might cease to unwarrantably obsess him—though of that last result he owned himself regrettably doubtful.

8
The Queen of Hearts

The main supper room of the Fifty-Three Limited ran through the entire building from front to back, and its decorations more nearly resembled those in the grill room of some luxurious English club than the lurid styles so often affected by New York night clubs. No futurist artist had been allowed free scope for a flamboyant talent, no Russian, Chinese or African influence appeared; instead, the place was sedately paneled in dark wood and furnished along three sides with small partly curtained stalls, with lights so discreetly shaded that their occupants might feel assured of almost complete privacy.

It was into one of these stalls that Tam and Calhoun were ushered by Davis, the proprietor, when the designated Joker with Fisk's name scrawled across it had duly admitted them to the club.

"May I ask a personal seconding of Lieutenant Fisk's guarantee that your visit is strictly unofficial?" he inquired when they were settled, his pasty, heavily dew-lapped face betraying a shade of the antagonism which he strove to hide.

"We're only here because of an interest in New York night life," Tam lied shamelessly, "and Lieutenant Fisk's request was made as a matter of friendship; it had no professional motive."

"Sorry to have troubled you, but just now, with feelings in both camps running so strong, it's necessary to be more than normally careful. Hope you will find the food to your taste, sir, and we run a first-class show beginning at midnight well worth waiting for; our artists are all A number 1."

"Nasty insect!" Tam observed when the "Joker" was safely out of hearing. "But if he's responsible for this club's creation he deserves some credit—it's rather a charming place."

Calhoun nodded agreement, then called her attention to the table between them.

"Notice the coloring? Lamp, flowers, table linen and china all to match, with most of the booths got up in varying shades; even the heads of the matches supplied follow the individual color scheme—quaint conceit, that last."

"All of which the patrons are duly fleeced for," Tam, who had been giving more attention to the occupants of the well-filled room than to its table decorations, retorted. "I can't see a sign of Rosamond. Do you suppose she's already left, or gone into some inner room?"

"Probably the latter; she'd hardly take so much trouble to get here unless she meant staying some time. What shall we have?" A waiter, menu card in hand, hovered awaiting their order.

"Oh, anything you like   "

When he made a slightly haphazard choice he turned back to find Tam absorbed in watching a woman, alone, who sat at one of the tables skirting the central dancing floor.

"Isn't she a gorgeous creature!"

Her open admiration for really beautiful members of her own sex was so frankly expressed that Calhoun inwardly chuckled; he had known so many women who resented admiration bestowed on anyone but themselves.

"It's Inga Farrar, just now starring in a Broadway musical comedy called 'The Flaming Tropics.'"

"The name might have been chosen for her especial benefit," Tam reflected aloud. "She looks like some hot, tropical blossom; but you must be wrong about her being in any show that's running now—she couldn't be here so early."

"Right. I expect the 'Flaming Tropics' has closed without my noticing. Wasn't much of a show, anyway," he added reminiscently. "Farrar was about the only worth-while thing in it and she's no voice to speak of but—she can dance!"

"Queer I've never seen or heard of her before."

"She's a bit of a new importation for New York, I believe. Broke into the show game in South America, and since then has mostly played the west coast; quite a following in California, so I understand."

"She should have, with beauty like that, if she's only a modicum of talent—still, it wasn't altogether her beauty that interested me. When I first noticed her, she was reading an evening paper with such absorption that a waiter had to touch her arm to attract attention."

"Probably inspecting the reports of the Stock Market."

"I think not—the page she was reading looked quite different, though of course she was too far away for me to see altogether clearly. I'm going to bribe our waiter to bring us the paper she's just tossed aside."

"Now why the deuce—?" Calhoun stared at her uncomprehendingly. "Why does it matter to you what section interests Farrar, when you admit never having heard of her?"

"I thought you claimed to have imagination; must I dot all my i's and cross my t's? But there, her expression had changed by the time you looked at her; she'd lost the look of one studying something that meant life or death."

"Seen the same hungry eagerness on many a face while its owner pored over the columns of stock prices quoted," he maintained. "After all, to the majority of humans there's nothing quite so vital as money."

"Cynic! And I ask you, does that face, with its fire and passion, suggest a mercenary brain behind it?"

Calhoun studied the dancer, who was now placidly eating a light supper. "If there's one thing I *have* learned about women, it's that you're never safe in trusting appearances. Take yourself, for example—who'd ever guess you to be a famous detective, with a most scandalous drag at police headquarters?"

"Well, you wouldn't have me running about in a tweed suit and horn-rimmed glasses, would you? Though that seems the conventional idea of how a woman detective ought to look. Here comes our waiter; will you ask him to get that particular paper, or shall I?"

"I shall."

When it was brought, Calhoun glanced at the article exposed by the last reader's folding, then showed it to Tam with a whimsical grin.

"Suppose you've already guessed—it concerned the Carew murder!"

"The picture looked familiar, but at that distance I couldn't be sure. Now, why is this musical comedy star so interested in our own private murder case?"

"Probably nothing more than morbid curiosity."

"Doubtful—the lady read with something more than impersonal curiosity, however avid. Can she know any of the principals the article deals with?"

"You've read it?"

"Yes. It contains nothing new, I mean nothing you don't already know."

"H-u-m-m—" His keen dark eyes skimmed over the printed columns. "There's a good bit about Rosamond

Forbes; somebody's been interviewing that man at the filling station."

"You think Farrar may know Rosamond?"

"Seems possible, since they both appear to frequent the
same night club. Hello, here's a new arrival who's headed
for Farrar's table, unless I'm much mistaken."

Tam, following his glance, saw a slender blonde, rather
showily and at the same time shabbily dressed who waved
to someone, then hastily passed their stall on her way to
the back part of the room; in the brief moment of passing
Tam had time to note that her delicate face had the same
lovely but ravaged look as her costume.

"Accurate guess," Tam approved as the newcomer sank
into an empty chair at Inga Farrar's table. "Partial to
blondes, that you stare so wholeheartedly?"

"Not to that world-weary type, but she looks vaguely
familiar. I can't for the life of me place her, though most
likely it's only a chance resemblance."

"They give the impression of acquaintances rather than
friends," Tam commented, still closely watching the two
women at the table. "Blonde seems to be making the ad-
vances—see how she leans across the table and how eagerly
she talks—brunette isn't having any; now she's signaling
for her check— Watch if she pays or signs, that will give
some indication of her standing here."

"Judging by blonde's frock, she's probably hard up and
trying to inveigle Farrar into paying for her supper."

It seemed a reasonable supposition, which the fact that
Inga Farrar hastily signed her supper check and rapidly
departed toward the cloak room with no more than the
briefest of goodnights to her table companion, did nothing to dispel.

"Shall we stay a bit longer on the chance of seeing
Rosamond, or shall we follow Miss Farrar and try to learn
if she's connected with our case?" Tam debated aloud.

"Why not toss a penny?" he suggested. "Either way's a pure gamble, no less."

"Not necessary, chance has already decided."

As she spoke, a section of the paneling near the big fireplace, which they had not hitherto suspected of being a door, slid aside, giving a glimpse of some inner, brilliantly lighted room, from which Rosamond Forbes slowly emerged. There was evidently no secret about the sliding panel, for none of the people near it paid the slightest attention to its opening or closing.

For a moment or two Rosamond, arrayed in one of the flaming red gowns she so much affected, stood picturesquely posed against the dark wood while she surveyed the now crowded supper room; then some signal or greeting brought a smile and answering gesture, as she moved quickly forward. Searching among the diners to see whence the signal had come, Tam and Calhoun saw the blonde whom Inga Farrar had so lately deserted standing up at her table, quite obviously waiting to welcome Rosamond. The two women met with almost sisterly enthusiasm, then sat down, heads close together, and fell into eager talk.

"No question about their intimacy." Tam's long, blue-grey eyes dwelt meditatively on them, while through her brain trooped a procession of unanswered questions.

Who was the faded, golden-haired woman whose now ravaged face must once have been very beautiful? What was her connection with Rosamond Forbes, and was it to see her that the latter had come to the club known as the Fifty-Three Limited?

"Singularly intimate for the Forbes woman." Oakley Calhoun unwittingly cut across the train of her thoughts. "The blonde looks positively down at heel."

"Yes, but I'm not so sure it's from lack of money; her general disarray looks more the result of carelessness than poverty. There's been no attempt at preserving appearances,

yet unless I'm wrong her dress is this season's model, an expensive one, and no woman could so soon reduce a gown to
that degree of shabbiness if she took half decent care of it."

"Wonder who she is? If you hadn't shown me Lydia
Carew's picture, I might half suspect the blonde was she."

"Why?"

"Perhaps because finding Lydia is our main object at
the moment, so I've rather got her on the brain; also a
little because this woman's coloring is much like Leslie's."

"Hardly sufficient, since she looks nothing at all like
the photograph we've both carefully studied. We must try
and learn who she is, and above all what club-card she's
known by, if any."

"Because?"

"Do you remember exactly what cards were found in
Leslie Carew's dead hand?"

"Afraid not," Calhoun admitted after a moment's re-
flection. "They didn't strike me as important."

"Until tonight I've been rather inclined to neglect them
myself. But since learning of the Fifty-Three Limited and
the part an ordinary playing deck takes in its membership,
I've realized how small things sometimes count. The cards
in Leslie's hand were: the Queen of Hearts, the Jack of
Spades, the Ace of Diamonds, one small card which I can't
remember, and the Joker."

"Not much of a poker hand—even with Jokers wild, the
best you could make would be a pair of aces."

Tam punished his flippancy with a repressive frown.
"Each of the four cards may—notice I only say, may—represent a Fifty-Three Limited member, of course supposing that whoever shot Leslie belonged to this club or was
in some way connected with it—in which case it's up to
us to discover who those other four cards represent. We
already know the Joker's identity; there seems no secret
about that."

"Where did the deck originally come from?"

"Property of the Meadow Dale Country Club—I did have sense enough to inquire about that at the time; don't forget, one of the cards I just mentioned has already cropped up somewhere else in the case."

"Haven't met it myself," he denied. "Not as a card. But how about that odd little inset in the murder-revolver?"

"Right! You said at the time it resembled an Ace of Diamonds."

"Only, knowing nothing of this club, I could only wonder whether the fact held any special significance. After tonight's developments I feel that discovering the identity of the Ace of Diamonds member may go a long way toward solving our mystery. The presence of both card and pistol can hardly be a coincidence."

"Hardly. But how do you propose locating the said Ace?"

"Haven't the faintest idea at present." Tam cheerfully alleged, accepting one of his offered cigarettes. Calhoun's lighter—quite in the irritating way of the breed—refused to work and after watching his struggles for a moment or so, Tam pushed over the match box, but, like most owners of patent lighters, he refused to be bested—there was no reason why the confounded thing shouldn't work. It finally did, with such unexpected vehemence that its flare resembled a small torch.

"Oh, damn!" Tam ejaculated with more sincerity than elegance. "You might just as well have lighted an electric torch and waved it about to attract Rosamond's attention!"

"Sorry!" he contritely apologized. "It doesn't usually blaze like that."

"Not necessary—once was enough. Now Rosamond will probably guess we're watching her. She knows us both by sight, worse luck."

"Can't we pretend we're here strictly for the purpose of flirtation? I can play the eager lover perfectly, if only you'll back me up."

"Well, I won't." She flatly declined. "In the first place I've had too little experience to do it convincingly, and in the second I don't imagine we'd deceive Rosamond— Too late anyway; she's rising and I believe she means joining us!"

"What's the idea?"

"Maybe wants us to think she's nothing to hide and has a perfectly tranquil conscience."

They had time for no more. Rosamond sailed into their stall with the haggard blonde in tow.

"When Mr. Calhoun lighted that violent flare, I couldn't help seeing you two and joining you!" She gushed with the utmost cordiality, covering, so Tam imagined, complete awareness and enjoyment of their chagrin. "Of course, Mr. Calhoun and I haven't been properly introduced, but we've met unofficially at the country club and the inquest, so I trust he'll forgive our lack of formality."

She did not wait for an invitation to appropriate one of the booth's extra chairs. "Nice club, don't you think? I'm a member, so quenching our midnight thirst is my affair." She beckoned a passing waiter and gave an order in a rapid undertone, which still reached the ears of the tired blonde.

"Only ginger ale for me, Rosamond. I don't want anything stronger."

"Nonsense, Queenie, a mint julep will buck you up and Lord knows you need it." Waving the waiter to hasten, she turned back to their involuntary hosts. "Miss—Hartson tried to obey the eighteenth Amendment, but we simply won't let her—a delicate constitution like hers needs a stimulant to keep it in proper working order. And now,

Miss O'Brien, please do tell us if you're here professional-
ly, or just on a spree?"

"More or less the last," Tam smilingly declared. "Even
a detective has to play about now and then, you know."

"I suspected you might be hunting for Lydia!"

"Why?"

"No particular reason, only you seemed so bent on
finding her, and I imagine you're rather a determined sort
of person."

"Well, since you belong to this club and yet haven't
seen Mrs. Chadwick in years, I think you said, looking for
her here would seem a pure waste of time."

"You mightn't have known that in advance," Rosamond
shrewdly observed, just as the waiter returned with four
tall frosty mint juleps, which proved, on sampling, very
good of their kind. "The Joker won't tell anybody where
he gets his stuff, but it's always excellent."

"More than I'd say for his cabaret show," the woman
whom Rosamond had introduced as Miss Hartson, contributed. "That contortionist dancer is simply awful. Her
legs look like white snakes."

Lydia Chadwick's name was not again mentioned, and
Tam and Calhoun departed as soon as they decently could,
leaving Rosamond and her "Queenie" in possession of
their stall.

"Feel the evening's drawn blank?" he inquired as Tam
settled at the wheel for the long run back to Meadow Dale.

"Not altogether. I think meeting Rosamond's blonde
friend was well worth our trouble—I intend visiting the
Fifty-Three Limited again and trying to cultivate her."

"For the love of Mike, why? She's a drearily uninterest-
ing sort and besides—"

"Yes?"

"I believe she's a drug addict."

"Nearly certain of it—that accounts for her appearance; they seldom take decent care of themselves or their clothes. But that wasn't what I meant."

"What then?"

"Rosamond called the woman 'Queenie,' whether by accident or design I'm uncertain; and not having much imagination, she introduced her as 'Miss Hartson'—an obviously false name, considering the enlightening pause while Rosamond thought it up. Rather suggests that the blonde is really known in the Fifty-Three Limited as the Queen of Hearts! And you'll remember that was one of the cards Leslie's hand held. So we can't say we've drawn entirely blank."

9

"Mrs. Jekyll-Hyde"

"I much prefer not discussing Leslie, indeed I can hardly do so with any unbiased fairness since I consider her directly responsible for my son's death."

Mrs. Carew spoke with a certain chill finality that might have discouraged a less determined seeker of information. But Tam O'Brien was not easily turned from a purpose. She had sought out the older woman with the fixed intention of persuading her into voicing her real opinion of Leslie Carew—believing that there were certain facts which the men who had known her were too chivalrous to mention, now that Leslie was dead.

"One or two people have hinted that your son's marriage was anything but happy. Yet, on the other hand, no one has given a specific reason, or implied any criticism of Leslie either as wife or social leader. Wouldn't it be fairer to Mr. Carew's memory to tell me exactly why their marriage wasn't a success?"

"Please don't suggest that the fault was my son's!" There was an undernote of passionate resentment in her levelly keyed voice. "Eric idolized his wife—he was peacock-proud of her beauty and popularity."

"Then why the friction, of which even their friends seem to have been aware?"

"It was largely a difference in tastes. My son cared for the society of his equals, he even enjoyed cards and wine in moderation—it was her abuse of both, together with her wild extravagance, which ruined his happiness."

"Surely he was wealthy enough to afford the most expensive of wives?"

"Oh, it was scarcely a question of actual expenditure," Mrs. Carew half impatiently explained. "Rather it was the excess to which Leslie carried all her fads and fancies. Pray don't misunderstand my meaning—I believe that Leslie, while possessing an insatiable appetite for masculine admiration, was technically faithful to her husband. But she had another side than the one seen by those friends who knew her only as a fastidious dictator of fashion, a leader who showed no mercy to any woman, such as Rosamond Forbes, whose reputation the taint of scandal had once blighted."

"May I infer that she led practically a double life?"

"Not quite that," Sarah Carew contradicted. "A few of her close intimates shared both phases; the ordinary intercourse of wealthy, well placed people, and the occasional descents into the wildest night life of the city. Gambling in any form held an irresistible fascination for my daughter-in-law, and I regret to say she sometimes drank more than discretion warranted. It was her spasmodic indulgence in such follies that broke Eric's heart."

"There was never a question of another?"

"Never!" Came the old lady's curt assertion, to be the next instant qualified with a hesitant "But—"

"Won't it be best to speak quite openly?"

"There is really almost nothing—" She hesitated, then plunged into the unrestrained confidences of the habitually reserved, once their inhibition against open speaking has been temporarily shattered. "During the last week of my son's life I was conscious of a growing tension—a barely restrained excitement that impregnated his every look and word. At the time I suspected some sort of crisis in his relations with Leslie, but of course I was utterly unprepared for his drastic taking of the end into his own hands. Even now I have no knowledge of what happened to make his life suddenly unbearable, but I'm convinced that Leslie was responsible for the trouble, whatever its exact pattern may have been."

"Has it ever occurred to you that, dearly loving his wife, the discovery that she had become a drug addict may have served as the last straw that broke his endurance?"

"No!" Mrs. Carew stared with a dawning horror. "No! That explanation has never crossed my mind."

"At present it's no more than a conjecture on my part," Tam hastened to assure her. "I hoped you might be able to confirm or refute it."

"Neither one. For the past three years, ever since Eric's death, in fact, Leslie and I have been practically strangers; only love for my grandson and his need of my care have kept us in the same house."

"You mean she was a neglectful mother?"

"At least an indifferent one. The child has never meant to her half what he has to me."

"In that case, her, engagement to Truxton Manning must have deeply grieved you."

"It did!" There was heart-felt sincerity in the older woman's voice. "They planned living permanently in California—the state where most of his interests center—which would have virtually meant my complete separation from my grandson."

"Was Leslie quite happy in her engagement?"

"So far as I know. In fact, I suspected that her love for Truxton Manning went far deeper than her affection for Eric had ever gone. Perhaps the wild streak underlying her nature found a kindred strain in his."

Tam allowed a brief silence to intervene between Mrs. Carew's last remark and her own next question; one which she put with a certain trepidation, fearing it might serve to rebuild the woman's normal wall of reserve.

"While working on a case we're bound to pick up all sorts of stray bits of probably valueless in formation. Among other such scraps, the fact that you and Leslie quarreled on the night of her death has turned up. I wonder if you could possibly tell me what about?"

"I fear not." A dash of embarrassed or resentful color stained Mrs. Carew's pale cheek? "It was a strictly personal matter."

"Something which could not be in any way connected with what happened later?"

"Ah!" It was a small, almost pained ejaculation. "I have sometimes waked in the night with the terrified thought that perhaps— But there, I'd better tell you! As you already know, for purely selfish reasons I hated the thought of Leslie's marriage to Truxton Manning; it meant the loss of my grandson. So, on the night of which you speak, I repeated to her some apparently authentic scandal concerning him which had reached my ears. It made her so furious, not only with me but with him as well, that I have sometimes wondered if he did not return unexpectedly soon, and, during the quarrel which would have been bound to follow their meeting in the mood she then was, become so enraged that he—that he—eternally silenced her!"

"You can safely dismiss that fear, Mrs. Carew. He was in Chicago on the night of Leslie's death."

"Yes, I know he says so, but are you sure? Remember how aircraft have annihilated distance!"

"The same thought occurred to me at first; since then I've learned that he dined and spent the evening up to past midnight with thoroughly reputable friends."

"Thank God! You have lifted an enormous weight from my mind, for I feared that by acquainting Leslie with Mr. Manning's relation to another woman, I had indirectly caused her death."

"Was the relation you speak of a thing of the past or present?" Tam cut in, hoping to surprise an answer before the other had time to think.

"Forgive me for refusing to answer—I have already said more than I should, since the facts were communicated to me in strict confidence, and they in no way concern her death."

"How can we be certain of that fact?"

"You just assured me Truxton Manning is known to have spent that night in Chicago."

"True. Yet that leaves the woman unaccounted for." Tam persisted, bent on learning all she possibly could.

"That scarcely matters—the scandal I mention dated from California days."

"And he has been east, how long?"

"Several months; I fear I can't tell you the exact number." Mrs. Carew's tone was suddenly abstracted and Tam, watching her, saw the sorrow-lined face and great mournful eyes soften and change under the stirring of some deep emotion; her own glance followed the older woman's and through the open window she saw a small boy romping gaily across the lawn, a dog at his heels. So—it was love for the child which had altered Sarah Carew almost past recognition! For the first time Tam understood Truxton Manning's conviction that she was capable of going to any lengths, even murder, in order to retain possession of her grandson.

There was another person on the lawn, a slight grayhaired figure that looked vaguely familiar. As boy and dog reached her and flung themselves upon her in almost equally demonstrative greeting, the woman turned toward the house and Tam recognized her.

"Isn't that the club stewardess, Dorcas—I'm afraid I've forgotten her surname."

"Dorcas Snell, yes. She was our housekeeper at the time baby was born, and has always retained a strong affection for him."

"It seems to be mutual," Tam remarked, as the boy pounded and pulled at Dorcas, quite unrebuked.

"She over-indulges him whenever we are here at Dune House. Being a native of Meadow Dale village, she came back here to live after her son's death, and of course we spend most of our summers here, have done so for years."

"I remember Dorcas once mentioned her son. You knew him?"

"Oh, yes. He was an odd contrast to his mother, a great tall boy, very handsome, as I remember."

Here all serious conversation was ended by little Bertie's tempestuous entrance into the room, sedately followed by the stewardess, and Tam soon left them. Her next visit was to Dr. Ramsey, upon whose afternoon office hours she trespassed without a qualm since his waiting room was patientless. Country air and summer weather had conspired to keep the Meadow Dale Colony in perfect health.

"Any news?" She settled into the comfortable chair he offered and lighted a cigarette, an indulgence which had seemed out of keeping with the Carews' formal drawing room.

"None at all." Dr. Ramsey's tone was a trifle guilty. He was conscious of having rather neglected the case, once the first novelty of officiating as coroner had worn off. "I've tried to trap Rosamond Forbes into admitting where she was between 9:30 and midnight, but without the slightest success."

"Sure your filling station witness is reliable?"

"Oh, certainly. I've known him all his life." The doctor responded as if that settled the matter once for all.

"Even reliable people sometimes make mistakes."

"No question of that here. He not only saw Rosamond, he talked to her while fixing the flat tire."

"And you still believe she killed Leslie, out of revenge for the latter's attitude about Rosamond's divorce?"

"Can you produce a more convincing motive?"

"Not at the moment, though I hope to in time."

"After all, it's not a pleasant thing to be cut off the receiving lists of most of your intimate friends," he defended his pet theory with a certain degree of heat, "and Rosamond has always possessed an extremely vicious temper."

"She doesn't seem particularly clever, but do you honestly think she's stupid enough to have advertised the lateness of the hour at which she was still out in her car, supposing she had just committed a daring murder?"

"I hadn't thought of that," he admitted with a slightly crestfallen air.

"Yet it's worth considering— Nothing's been heard of Lydia Chadwick, I suppose?"

"No, though Leslie's will has been probated and its provisions widely printed; she has only to come forward, to claim and receive that thirty thousand."

"And incidentally walk straight into the waiting arms of the narcotic agents? You seem to forget she and her husband are both wanted for illicit drug traffic! By the way, I have a picture supplied by Rosamond Forbes—sorry I haven't it here; I'd like to get your opinion of the likeness. You knew Lydia well?"

"Naturally. Being an old intimate of the family I've known both girls since babyhood."

Tam eyed the doctor intently. Then, with careful casualness, she asked:

"Returning to the subject of drugs: Am I wrong in thinking Leslie Carew was a victim of the habit?"

"Why— How—" He stared at her with obvious consternation. "What put such an idea into your head?"

"I notice you don't deny it. As for my reasons: Doctor, I thought you held something back at the inquest. Since then, one or two things have made me suspect the thing you held back was Leslie's use of drugs."

Dr. Ramsey paused, clearly in much embarrassment.

"I felt nothing was to be gained by damaging her good name and inflicting further sorrow on her family. . . . Of course Leslie's use of morphine had nothing to do with her murder."

"That remains unproven. Was she what is technically known as a 'snowbird'—one who sniffs the stuff—or did she use an hypodermic?"

"The last. Her thighs told the whole story. I suppose there was less danger of the needle-marks being seen there, than on her arms."

"Should you say, judging by the scars left, that it was a recently formed habit?"

The doctor was speaking frankly now. He seemed relieved.

"No. I should say one of old standing, though of course the older scars had faded considerably with the passing of time. Why are you interested?"

"Because," said Tam, "one who uses dope often leads a Jekyll-Hyde life.—Just one more question and I'll leave you in peace. Have you seen Truxton Manning since the inquest?"

"Only a few times. You know he's left Dune House and is staying at some New York hotel. To be perfectly honest, Manning's attitude rather puzzles me. You remember how eager he was at first, how he openly declared his suspicion that Sarah Carew had shot Leslie to prevent her taking the child away?" Tam merely nodded, and Dr. Ramsey hurried on. "Since the inquest, he seems to have lost all interest in the solving of the crime. He even shows a wish to let the whole matter drop. And when I mentioned his former suspicion against Sarah Carew, he tried his best to retract it—mumbled about his brain having been overheated by the sudden shock, and that what people said under intense emotional strain shouldn't be taken too seriously."

"Something happened at the inquest that radically changed Manning's viewpoint. Only wish I could guess what it was."

"Surely there were no startling developments, no new evidence to account for his abrupt about-face."

"Yet some fact *was* brought out," she insisted. "Or perhaps something that had no direct bearing on the inquest itself. He may have heard news or gossip of which we're quite ignorant, say from someone in the audience. I'll never feel satisfied until I know what it was."

"Why not ask Manning?"

"He doesn't strike me as the sort to receive unwelcome questions in a kindly spirit—still if I have an opportunity I'll probably do just that."

"What did you mean by a 'Jekyll-Hyde life'?" queried Dr. Ramsey. "You used that phrase a moment ago. I'm your pupil in these matters, Miss O'Brien. Won't you enlighten me?"

"Dr. Jekyll was respectable, honored, fine—Mr. Hyde was just the opposite," Tam explained. "Yet they were the same person. The change in character resulted from the use of drug. The story has a real-life basis—and the drug is morphine! Doctor, Leslie Carew was a woman of social position and charm. But in her phase of dope addict, who knows what friends she had, what things she did? She might have been a 'Mrs. Jekyll-Hyde'—at any rate it's worth investigating."

Tam let the doctor return to his interrupted nap, and strolled across to the country club in search of Scanlan,

its head steward. Scanlan was only too glad to break the
tedium of a long midweek afternoon by answering as many
questions as Tam chose to put, but none of them helped in
the slightest. She left the club for her boarding place no
whit wiser than on her arrival.

Halfway home she met Dorcas Snell, a covered basket
over one arm. The woman stopped her with a timid question:

"I didn't like to ask you at Dune House, Miss, but have
you found out who killed Mrs. Leslie?"

"Not yet, Dorcas, in fact we're a long way from knowing."

"Please forgive my asking, but it's not just curiosity—I
was the Carew housekeeper for so long that it's almost a
personal matter with me."

"Mrs. Carew told me you were with them when the
baby was born. Did you stay long afterwards?"

"Oh, yes, Miss. I didn't leave until some time after Mr.
Eric's death."

"Then perhaps you can tell me about the last few days
or weeks of his life?"

"About them, Miss? I'm afraid I don't understand."

"Surely Mr. Carew wasn't quite his normal self during
those last few days. You must have realized that he was
deeply troubled, unhappy—didn't you form some opinion
as to the cause?"

"If I did, it's so long ago I've forgotten. Looking back
I can't remember seeing anything unusual about Mr. Eric.
He was always unhappy, you know, Miss; just couldn't
seem to get on with his wife."

"They quarreled?"

"Oh, no, Miss, never that!" Dorcas sounded distinctly
shocked. "They were much too well bred for that! But Mr.
Eric used to talk to his wife by the hour on end, sort of
gentle and pleading, trying to persuade her into giving up

things he didn't like her to do—then, after he'd talked and
talked, she'd give a taunting little laugh and run out of the
room as gay as you please, to call up some of her friends
and start another party. What Mr. Eric said never seemed
to make the smallest difference to her; she just went her
own way regardless."

"He never tried more forcible measures?"

"Mrs. Leslie was never one you could force into anything, Miss. She'd a great fondness for doing as she liked."

"And you're sure you know of nothing to account for
Mr. Carew's taking his own life?"

"Perfectly sure. I've often wondered just why he did it,
but I've never been able to decide that it wasn't just getting too tired to struggle any more."

"There must have been some different reason, I think,
but now Leslie is dead we may never know it."

"I'm sorry I couldn't help you, Miss," Dorcas apologized. "But a housekeeper doesn't see anything like as
much of what goes on as, say, a lady's maid does—Anice
might know something I don't."

"Thanks for the hint! I believe I'll ask her."

But at the moment the precise cause of Eric Carew's
suicide appeared to have no bearing on their investigation,
so Tam pigeon-holed the matter for future inquiry, and
on reaching the cottage went up to her own room to make
ready for a swim. She rapidly changed into her bathing
suit, then began frantically searching for the long wrap
which her landlady had evidently secreted in some new
hiding place, not with the least intention of irritating her
lodger but simply because to a tidy habit of mind she added an incurably short memory, and almost never put any
article away twice in the same place.

This time the wrap was bestowed in a lower drawer
where it had no business to be, and as Tam impatiently
yanked it out, a square of cardboard came with it; the

photograph of Lydia Chadwick, which had been supplied by Rosamond Forbes. Tam had thrust it into the privacy of a drawer generally kept locked. She picked it up and stood studying the pretty smiling face.

Should she ever be able to find the original, and if she did how much would it help? Rather a singular way for one girl to sign a likeness given to another only the one word "Lydia," with no term of greeting or endearment—yet they had been intimate friends at the time.

"OH!"

Abruptly Tam carried the photograph to the window for closer inspection. She had noticed a fact hitherto over-looked. In her absorption in the face itself, she had rather neglected the brief signature, failing to realize that it was written with a very black pencil, not ink.

Now, why a pencil? Unless the look of an inked signature would not have corresponded to the supposed date of its writing!

With the tiny green light that danced in Tam's eyes when some new clue gave added zest to her work, suddenly aflame, she threw her thoughts back to the night of Leslie Carew's death and her own search of Room 14, where Leslie had supped with a single mysterious guest. Those initials carelessly traced on the table cloth—could she succeed in remembering the precise formation of that scrawled "L"?

Not quite, perhaps—but nearly enough to be certain the "L" in the name signed across Lydia Chadwick's supposed picture was of an utterly different type.

So Rosamond Forbes was not so stupid after all! She had apparently palmed off an old photograph of some other girlhood friend, claiming it to be a portrait of Lydia Chadwick! Her object was easily enough guessed; while Tam hunted the original of that picture, the real Lydia might safely sail under the detective's very nose with little fear of her identity being suspected.

Perhaps she had already so sailed—and suddenly Tam relieved her feelings by a laugh of sheer amusement. She was Irish enough to enjoy a joke even at her own expense, and suppose—just suppose—that Rosamond had last night calmly introduced the true Lydia Chadwick to Tam and Calhoun, secure in the safety afforded by that deceiving picture!

Well, if Lydia Chadwick and the Fifty-Three Limited's Queen of Hearts were one and the same, that blonde suddenly became a person of very vital interest. Better send a note around to Oakley Calhoun, suggesting another excursion to the night club that very evening.

10

A Dancer's Love

They had little trouble gaining admission to the Fifty-Three Limited, as the door man remembered them from the previous night and Calhoun gave the required signals without a flaw.

Upstairs, the long supper room was so full that most of the booths were already taken, but Tam firmly refused the waiter's suggestion of a table in the open.

"No. I see a friend in one of the farther stalls; we'll ask if we may not join her."

The "friend" to whom she referred was the Queen of Hearts, sitting quite alone in one of the end booths. She seemed unaware of their approach until Tam actually addressed her, then half rose with a startled, almost frightened exclamation and a momentary spasmodic trembling that betrayed her drug slavery even more plainly than did her lovely, ravaged face.

"Forgive me, I was dreaming—" She stammered, unable instantly to regain self-control. "Won't you—please do sit down."

"Beg a thousand pardons, Madame," apologized a flurried head waiter. "But this stall is reserved—I was told to keep it empty, once madame had finished her supper."

Calhoun regarded him from beneath drooped lids. "The next booth is vacant, why not shift your reservation to that?"

"Oh, it's much simpler for us all to move in there."
The still trembling Queen of Hearts fell to hastily gathering her scattered possessions—dropping first gloves, then
vanity case, in her anxious haste; but Calhoun was unaccustomed to accepting dictation, and calmly refused to
establish a new precedent.

"Pray don't permit yourself to be disturbed, Miss Hartson," he urged. "Besides, the color scheme of the next
booth would clash with the frock you're wearing—these
chaste white decorations form an effective background and
the violent green next door would do nothing of the sort."

"I can have another booth emptied." The waiter offered, still determined to prevent their occupancy of that
especial place. "Madame can choose which color she likes,
lavender, blue, rose—"

"But not white?" Calhoun cut in.

"I am desolated." The man's hands went out in a gesture of helpless apology. "All the white booths seem already taken."

"Then we can't resign this one. White has always been
my favorite color."

"Only, you know, it isn't a color," Tam reminded him
while the waiter, succumbing to the inevitable as represented by Calhoun's habit of getting his own way, helped
them to settle comfortably in the disputed stall.

"Now, I wonder what lay behind all that fuss?" Tam
reflected aloud as the discomforted head waiter retired to
pass their order on to some lesser light of the table service.

"Some of the older members like to have a particular
place reserved for them." The Queen of Hearts explained
with unconcealed disapproval.

"Surely another stall would have done just as well."

"Not unless it was decorated in white." She flung him a
furtive, almost venomous look, then caught at her ebbing
temper and forced a smile.

"Let's hope you enjoy your triumph, though I can't stay to witness it."

"Surely you won't desert us—innocent strangers within your gates?" he protested, a hint of mockery in his laughing black eyes.

"Well, not instantly; I'll at least stay for another cigarette." She selected one from her own case, ignoring his. "Please pass the matches, they're just beyond my reach."

"Pardon me, I'm inexcusably clumsy—let me offer you a light from my individual fire-box instead." In reaching for the requested matches, he had managed to awkwardly push them over the table edge so that they fell to the floor—close to his feet. As soon as her cigarette was alight he stooped, apparently bent on recovering them, but straightened after a moment's futile groping. "They've fallen out of my reach; odd how dropped articles usually snuggle into inaccessible corners. Fortunately my lighter's in good working order tonight."

When their order arrived, the Queen of Hearts accepted some wine, slowly sipping it while she chatted, a trifle at random of nothing in particular, presently lapsing into a silence that made Tam wonder why she lingered; it was almost as if, for some reason, she feared to leave them alone. Perhaps a half hour went by, during the latter part of which Tam and Calhoun talked, their guest saying nothing at all, then the woman suddenly awoke to electrified life—a muted cry drew their startled attention so that both saw her rise, hands outflung in a half frantic repulsion, a pushing back of some approaching danger, while her eyes widened so that a white rim showed around the entire iris.

Tam whirled to see what had so terrified her. But there seemed nothing in the length of the long room to account for her obvious horror. Next instant the Queen of Hearts sank back into her chair, one trembling hand across her eyes.

"What is it?" Calhoun demanded with the asperity usually displayed by men in the presence of a woman's unexplained fear.

"Not—anything," She let her hand drop, staring at him almost blankly. "My nerves are all wrong—hallucinations—sometimes I see what isn't really there."

"And just now?" he persisted.

"A sort of vision—there behind your shoulder—I think I'd better go."

They made no attempt to dissuade her, but when she had gone they consulted one another with questioning eyes.

"Think it was just the effect of morphine?" he inquired.

"No, I think she really saw something or someone—perhaps she was actually warning that someone away."

"H-m-m—her look would certainly have warned any-one behind us against closer approach, if that was what she was really doing instead of indulging a personal fear. Here comes Inga Farrar—do you suppose it could have been she whom the Queen of Hearts saw?"

"Oh, no." Tam dismissed the suggestion as not worth considering, then turned to look at the dancer, who was sitting down at one of the floor tables not far from their booth. "She's expecting someone; see, the waiter's filling both water glasses. Why—it's Truxton Manning!"

The big oil millionaire sat down at Inga Farrar's table so that both were seen from their stall in profile.

"Seeking quick consolation for Leslie's loss," was Calhoun's slightly disgusted comment.

"No, I don't think it's that." She quietly contradicted. "He hasn't the air of a man bent on conquest, in fact." She grinned at him with an edge of mockery. "If I didn't know, I'd put them down as a long-married couple, he's so serenely detached and uninterested in her comfort—obviously thinking of something else."

"Mean to insinuate the husband who's been such any length of time always neglects his wife's comfort?" he indignantly demanded.

"Oh, not intentionally; her likes and dislikes have ceased to be of the first importance, that's all. Now, honestly, did you ever see a husband gaze fondly into his own wife's eyes with the rapt, lost-dog sort of expression the old person on your left is directing toward his dainty supper guest?"

"Certainly I have!" Calhoun maintained, after a furtive glance in the direction indicated, where a white-haired, rotund old gentleman was neglecting his own supper in favor of fatuously watching his perhaps twenty-year-old companion heartily enjoy hers.

"Liar! You know perfectly well it isn't done. Rather surprising—Manning's friendship for the dancer, I mean, not the average husband's indifference."

"Don't they both hail from California? Perhaps they met there."

"Very possible. I wonder—"

"Irritating habit some people have, of leaving a sentence half in the air."

"I was only wondering if Inga Farrar can be the other woman Mrs. Carew mentioned," she explained. "If she is, there's another person we ought to watch. Too bad we're not half a dozen instead of only two; there'd be enough work on this case to keep us all busy."

"Speaking of watching, why didn't we trail the Queen of Hearts?"

"I phoned in her description to an assistant of mine— imagine he'll successfully pick her up when she leaves the club and besides I'm more interested in finding the Ace of Diamonds."

"We sound like a couple of professional gamblers," Calhoun laughed. "Any idea how to locate the elusive Ace?"

What could upset Queenie so that she gave the impression she was in terror of her life?

"More or less." She was still studying the two at the nearby table. "They haven't seen us, I think."

"No. Manning seems too wrapped in his own thoughts, and as for the fair Inga, well, there's no wifely indifference showing in her manner—she's eyes only for him."

"Sad but true," Tam conceded. "If ever a woman's eyes revealed slavish devotion, hers are doing it now. They're old friends, too; notice how she sugared his coffee without asking the amount he liked, and how she placed the salt and paprika within easy reach, but not the black pepper? Evidently she's familiar with his tastes."

"Strong on observing the small indications, aren't you?"

"A detective has to be. Generally the little things tell much more than the big ones and they're also less watched over by those harboring intent to deceive. Though in this particular case, Inga's face alone is enough to remove all doubt as to her love for Manning; there's no need to watch for secondary signs."

"The pair of them seems to be pretty well absorbing you," he complained, his voice holding an edge of jealousy that caused Tam an inward chuckle of amusement.

"We're not here to hold a mutual admiration meeting," she reminded him, "but to try and solve the mystery of Leslie's murder."

"I never before realized how delightful a murder investigation could be. Only hope it strings on for weeks."

"Nice of you, I'm sure, considering that I'm a hard-working detective whose time means money." She stopped, level brows knitting in a perplexed frown. "Inga is going to the ladies' room—wonder if I'd better risk Manning's seeing me by following her and trying to scrape an acquaintance?"

"We're so close, he's almost bound to see us anyway."

"That's true—think I'll risk it."

She found Inga Farrar applying lip rouge to her beautiful sullen mouth; her eyes watching the process with an odd detachment. "Only habit," was Tam's thought, "she doesn't really care how she looks tonight—probably feels Manning won't actually see her." Then, after a search of her hand-bag:

"I wonder if you'd loan me a match? I seem to have left mine outside."

"Surely." Inga proffered the desired light, and the two pairs of eyes, sultry black and cool blue-gray, looked into something more significant than a casual meeting—it was as if each guessed Life meant flinging them into some close relation, whether of friendship or enmity neither knew.

"You came here in search of me," the dancer asserted. "Why?"

"Only to this room, not to the club." Tam felt a strange compulsion to yield those imperiously demanding eyes the literal truth—to be the next instant cloaked by an evasion. "You're supping with a man who interests me."

"Truxton Manning?"

"Yes."

"Why should his movements concern you?"

"I may as well tell you, since if I don't he will. I'm a detective, engaged in trying to unravel the mystery surrounding his fiancée's death."

The test word "fiancée" drew a wave of pained crimson across the dancer's cheeks, to be instantly drained away by some succeeding thought.

"There is no possible reason to suspect Truxton!" she panted. "He was not here, not in New York, at the time!"

"Have I said I suspected him?"

"No, but—why else are you watching him?"

"It's only incidental," Tam assured her. "All Leslie Carew's former intimates are sharing the honor."

"Then you're actually ignorant of who killed her?"

"At least you've read of no arrests in the case," Tam parried.

"Oh, please don't fence with me!" The musical voice throbbed with a passionate pleading. "If you only knew what his safety means—yet there is some danger hanging over him—I can feel it, I, who have studied his every mood, learned to read his slightest change of expression—I know there is something which he terribly fears."

"If that's true, I can only swear I've no idea what it is. Perhaps you mistake his grief over Leslie Carew's loss for something else."

"No. Of course he might claim it was that, but I know better; he's far too selfish to grieve deeply over the loss of any woman."

"If you think him selfish, callous, why worry over what's troubling him?"

Inga flung her a glance of blighting contempt. "Much you know of love, if you think a woman can shut off anxiety simply because the man she worships is selfish, or much worse! I can't break the habit of living only for and through him—even though he has tired."

"Do you quite realize what you're saying?"

"Perfectly! I've never been ashamed of belonging to Truxton Manning, I've been proud of it—should be proud, now, to go back to him, if only he wanted me." Such burning devotion was beyond the ken of Tam's cooler, saner nature. Yet she felt no doubt regarding the genuine depth of Inga's openly declared emotion, and, as the French say, "It gave her furiously to think." Here was a possibility not hitherto considered.

"Why do men so seldom appreciate single-hearted devotion?" Tam spoke as if from a wealth of personal experience. "The more we love them, the sooner they tire."

"Of course!" The shining black head nodded a convinced agreement. "Once the thrill of conquest is passed and they know us their willing slaves, where is the zest?

But me, I was even more stupid—I let him see I was jealous! And that always throttles the poor remnants of a man's love."

"He left you when he grew interested in Leslie Carew?" Tam ventured the question, sure she would never again catch the dancer in such a communicative mood.

"Oh, long before that—in California. I had belonged to him for two years and then I let myself grow too sure. I made claims, as no woman with an atom of sense should ever do. Naturally that was fatal, he felt me a burden and left me—oh, but with a very generous settlement." Her laugh was wormwood bitter. "When will men learn that a full purse can't atone for an empty heart?"

"You followed him to New York?"

For a second Inga hesitated, then answered: "Yes. I told myself it wasn't so—that I was simply accepting a good professional offer—but in my heart I knew the real motive was hunger to see Truxton again."

"You knew of his engagement?"

"Not then. Later I read of it."

"And of course you tried to see him, to ask if it was really true?"

"No. I knew him much too well, knew what reception I'd get. I never saw him until one night in the theater in my dressing room—after she was dead. Then it was *he* who came to *me!* He wanted only friendship, nothing else; of course I gave him what he wished, glad at simply being with him, hearing his voice again after the long silent months, and in some way my companionship seemed to ease the trouble that's been preying on his mind. I haven't dared put a question—yet I know there is some black fear hanging over his head!"

"Haven't you gained even a hint as to what it is?"

The question was destined to remain unanswered. A low but insistent knocking on the door made Inga flash across to answer it; all her movements were astonishingly rapid. Outside stood an apologetic waiter.

"A thousand pardons; the gentleman sent me to inquire if madame was ill, that she remained so long away."

"Which gentleman?" With a questioning glance toward Tam.

"Yours, Madame, the gentleman known as—"

"Hush!" Inga hissed the word almost venomously. "We do not mention the name of any card before strangers. Tell him I'll return at once." She closed the door and stood, her back against it, facing Tam. "Have I been a fool to speak so openly—have I caused you to eye him with suspicion?"

"Certainly not." Tam answered with perfect truth. "On the contrary, you've made me look in quite a different direction."

"Thank God!" And she was gone, her departure accomplished with the speed that seemed one of her most marked characteristics.

Back at their own table, Tam sank into her place with a relieved sigh. "Heavens! If volcanic emotions are so exhausting to the onlooker, what must they be to their possessors?"

"Meaning exactly what?" Calhoun interestedly inquired.

She rapidly repeated the gist of what had passed between Inga and herself. "Opens new possibilities, doesn't it?"

"With a vengeance! A jealous, fire-blooded creature such as you describe would be perfectly capable of shooting a successful rival."

"Yes, but—" Tam paused, mentally going back over the scene in the dressing room. "If guilty, she's a superb actress—her whole anxiety appeared to center on Manning."

"Clever of her. She knows he's a water-tight alibi. They're getting ready to leave—probably her report of the conversation spoiled his appetite."

"Glad of it," she retorted with a trace of almost personal resentment. He deserves to be upset after the way he's treated Inga!"

"Most and generally, there are two sides to every story," he impartially informed her. "In this case you've heard only one."

"How like a man!" Then she laughed with a return to her normal good-temper. "I'm beginning to suspect there may be a grain of truth in Mac's contention that I'm too much influenced by feminine beauty."

"And who, may I ask, is Mac?"

"Inspector McCoy, whom you met last night at headquarters."

"Oh!" His tone was distinctly relieved. "I imagine no one would deny the beauty of this particular lady, but I'll admit being more interested in her possible guilt. She may, you know, be the missing Ace of Diamonds."

"Equally, so may Truxton Manning! I'd give something to know what card the waiter would have named if Inga hadn't stopped him. Aside from her possible identity as the Ace of Diamonds, there are one or two other items worth considering. Remember how, when you talked with Jones, the Meadow Dale taxi driver, the thing that most impressed him about his unknown fare on the night of the club dance was the extreme rapidity with which she moved?"

"Yes."

"Watching Inga tonight, I realized she habitually moves with a lithe swiftness I've never seen anyone else display—it's so marked, even an unobservant person could hardly fail to notice it."

"You're suggesting that she was Jones' passenger that night—the passenger who dropped, then recovered, a pistol as she left the car?"

"Seems possible, don't you think?" Adding, a second later: "No, I'm wrong. The club dance was on a Friday night, and you say Inga Farrar has been playing in a Broadway show—unless it closed week before last she can't have been in Meadow Dale at the time of Leslie's death."

"We'll inquire tomorrow and find out just when *The Flaming Tropics* did close. Anything more we can do tonight?"

"Not here. I'm hoping to get a report concerning the Queen of Hearts as we go out."

11

Above the Embankment

On the pavement outside, Tam looked in vain for the small figure of the assistant whom she had phoned to shadow a certain carefully described blonde; he was probably still on the trail. They went toward Tam's car, parked half down the block, but before reaching it were overtaken by a man in uniform, breathless for hurrying.

"Beg pardon, are you Mr. Oakley Calhoun?" he panted, then, at Calhoun's nod of assent, produced a slightly crumpled note. "I'm from the Flower Hospital—a friend of yours, name of Fitzharris, is there, badly smashed up in an accident. In fact, there's not much hope of his living and he's begging to see you before the end. I've a car waiting—if you hurry, we may be in time."

Instead of rushing to answer the summons Calhoun calmly asked a question: "What's that in your hand?"

"A note from your friend," the uniformed man muttered. "I forgot to hand it over, because I'm conscious that every second's delay lessens your chance of seeing him alive."

"Badly smashed up, dying, yet able to write notes; h-m-m!" was Calhoun's cryptic comment. "Let's have a look." He deliberately smoothed out the crumpled sheet, examining it by the light of the nearest street lamp.

"One of the doctors guided his hand, I believe," the messenger explained.

"Quite so—guided it so efficiently that there's no resemblance to Fitzharris' usual script. You and I'd better do a little talking before—"

But the uniformed messenger had not lingered to hear the end of the sentence. He was off down the block, running like a racing greyhound. Calhoun made a quick move of pursuit, then changed his intention or perhaps curbed the impulse, and turned to the watching Tam.

"A bit crude in their methods—maybe depended on rushing me away before I'd time to think!"

"But why?" Tam perplexedly inquired as they climbed into the waiting roadster. "And how did you instantly know the message was a fake?"

"To answer the last question first: Fitzharris couldn't possibly have known where to find me. He was out sailing when I got your note suggesting tonight's expedition and hadn't returned when I left, nor did I leave word as to where I'd gone. Also, that uniform wasn't the kind worn in hospitals by either orderlies or internes; and when I heard that, though fatally hurt, Fitzharris was still able to write notes, my last doubt vanished. Not that I entertained many from the start. As to why someone tried to drag me off on a wild goose chase—I'm afraid they wanted to separate us, wanted to get you alone."

"You really think that?" Her tone was so pleased that Calhoun glared at her as the car sped smoothly along a cross-town street.

"Why so cheery at the thought?"

"Because if you're right, the trail must be hotter than I'd realized! If I wasn't closing in on someone, they'd have no reason to want me removed."

"And, of course, only the murder chase matters, not your personal safety?"

"No need of waxing sarcastic about it." She flung him a friendly side glance. "If my safety, as you call it, was of paramount importance, I wouldn't be a detective; I'd be sitting tranquilly at home reading sex novels and playing contract bridge like the average well-behaved young female."

"Oh, they have other amusements," he laughed, adding with abrupt gravity; "How did you ever happen to select the detection of crime as a profession, anyway? I've puzzled over it ever since I knew you."

"Runs in the blood, I suppose," she told him with a seriousness that matched his own. "My father was for years connected with the Metropolitan Police Force, and before he retired was a much-loved Chief of Detectives. Mother died when I was very small, so he and his cronies practically brought me up—I heard them discussing whatever case chanced to be absorbing the attention of the force, before I could read.

"As I grew older, Dad used to like telling me about his cases, detailing all the evidence, partly because going over it at length helped him to get a proper prospective, partly because he claimed my fresher point of view often picked out the vital importance of some fact or clue which he'd practically lost sight of amid the accumulated mass of evidence. If I'd been a boy, I suppose under such training I'd have joined the force as soon as I was old enough. My sex forbidding that, I still couldn't separate myself from the ranks of those who spend their lives struggling to eliminate crimes and criminals. So—here I am, a private inquirer. Not that the work doesn't, incidentally, pay very well," she ended on a sudden lighter note.

"Doesn't your father object?"

"On the contrary, he enjoys helping on some of my cases. My work, and the advice he often gives, save him from brain-rust."

"But the frightful risks you run—a woman tracking down the most desperate criminals!"

"Still harping on that note?" She laughed softly. "Dad gives me credit for knowing how to take care of myself. Besides, through him I've the friendship of the entire police force to fall back on in time of need."

Calhoun, silenced, but quite unconvinced, retired into a thoughtful reverie; a building of air-castles in which he persuaded her to resign her dangerous profession in favor of the age-old one of homebuilder. They had reached the open Long Island road when he was roused by the frantic barking of a motorcycle close behind them.

"Hello! Some of your friends after us?"

The motorcycle whizzed by at a pace that ignored all speed limits.

"Certainly not. The police only go like that when they're bent on overtaking some car—too bad there's not one of them about now, to stop that maniac."

The thread of his dreaming once broken, Calhoun remembered certain facts and suspicions that he had not yet passed on to Tam. He dug into an outer coat pocket and produced an innocent looking box of matches, holding them out for her inspection.

"Thanks, I don't want to smoke just now," she told him, mistaking the significance of the gesture.

"If you did, these particular matches wouldn't help you to a light—it's the box of white-headed ones which the Queen of Hearts tried to prevent my examining."

"The ones from our table? So they weren't as completely lost as you pretended."

"They were calmly reposing in my pocket while I accused them of having taken refuge in a corner. Perhaps you didn't catch the lady's expression when she first started to leave us in possession of the booth then decided to stay for a final cigarette—the way she looked at those matches, before asking me to pass them, told it was on their account she stayed. That's why I knocked them off and afterwards pretended I couldn't find them."

"Afraid you've got me beyond my depths," she confessed. "Won't you please elucidate?"

"Well, to start at the beginning, I got the impression last night that there was something peculiar about the finicky attention paid to the color schemes in the club stalls. Why have such variety of color, when one or two that harmonized would give a better effect? I didn't mention the idea to you because of its vagueness; instead, I kept an eye on the booths' occupants and watched to see what types among the club patrons favored certain colors. Now, there are eight or ten different shades used, but I soon found two of them were differently treated from the rest—only the head waiter himself assigned anyone to the booths decorated in white, or those of combined black and yellow; the single instance by the bye, in which two colors are used. Last night I couldn't hit on an answer to the riddle, but when both head waiter and Queen of Hearts were so insistent on removing us from that white stall, I guessed the key must lie under my hand if I could only grasp it; her interest in the match box proved what that key was.

"While you were in the dressing room with Inga Farrar, I unobtrusively scraped off a flake or two of the white matchhead and tasted it. No mistaking the flavor, once you know it—they're made of cocaine."

"Clever work!" Tam applauded. "I saw you were interested in the table decorations, but was too eagerly watching what went on outside our booth for the fact to register. But go on, you've something else up your sleeve."

"Only concerning the black and yellow stalls. Having been so much in the Orient, I'm familiar with the look of opium users and while I haven't tested the theory I imagine those particular booths have black-headed matches formed of opium. The people frequenting them all wore the marks of the poppy-addict.

"On the face of it, the club's scheme of so openly supplying their patrons with the desired drug seems infernally risky, but second thought shows there's a lot to recommend it. It eliminates any actual handing over of the drugs; probably the addicts simply help themselves to the desired amount, and the price is added to their supper checks with no comments passed and no drugs mentioned—of course all the club waiters are in on the plan."

"Yes, and in case of a sudden raid it's ten to one the matches wouldn't be noticed; while even if they were, it would be difficult to prove the management knowingly supplied them. Oh," a sudden note of acute distress, "it's a crime that we've promised not to turn in a report on the club at headquarters—in fairness we can't even drop a hint!"

"Don't you ever think of anything more personal than your detective work?" Calhoun rather wistfully inquired.

"Not very often. To do anything well you must give your whole mind to it—don't you think?"

"Oh, I can quite understand one subject engrossing a person's entire mind," he responded feelingly. "But it would have to be something more intimate than the pursuit of evil-doers. Ever tried turning your attention to a—ahem—side issue like love?"

Instead of answering, Tam applied the brakes with such startling suddenness that he barely escaped being flung through the windshield.

"Lord! Is that the way the word 'love' affects you!" He laughed as the roadster came to an abrupt stop.

Ignoring his flippancy, she sprang lightly out and walked toward an upright white-painted sign bearing the legend: "Keep to the right." Calhoun, mystified, hardly knew whether to follow her or to stay where he was, but a moment later she called back to him in an odd, rather shaken voice.

"Bring the torch from the door pocket and come here!"

Just at that point the road swung sharply to the left, running along the top of a steep embankment, and the sign at which Tam stared was so placed on the outer edge of the curve, that anyone following its instruction must inevitably plunge over the embankment lip; a sheet drop of at least twenty feet.

"You see what's been done? Driving to the right of that sign would mean unavoidable disaster!"

"How did you guess?"

"As the headlights struck the sign, I realized it wasn't genuine—it's no more than a hastily executed copy of the real one. Look!" She pointed to an upright dark shape in the road's true center. "They hadn't time to remove the actual sign—you know they're firmly set in a concrete base—so they muffled it in something dark, trusting we'd only catch the white of their substitute."

"God, what a hellish scheme! You think it was planned for our benefit?"

"Mine, I'm afraid—that's why, having no particular grudge against you, they tried to get you away. And don't forget, it must have been engineered by someone knowing the intimate relations of the whole Meadowdale group. Otherwise they'd not be aware that Fitzharris is your closest friend. It's cleverly planned, though," she added with unresentful admiration. "They selected a spot where the tree-shadows fall across the road, helping to hide the genuine sign. It was only the merest chance, my noticing the substitution; being familiar with this road, I knew there was a sign of that type here—it was put up not long ago because people *would* hug the wrong side of the curve and there've been several accidents."

"But—do you realize any innocent motorist might have taken the plunge before we came along? How could they be sure we'd be the first comers after the stage was set?"

"Probably someone was hidden among the trees, ready to stop any other car."

Calhoun cast an apprehensive glance at the trees in question. "If that's true, what's to prevent the watcher taking a pot-shot at you now? We'd better clear out."

"Not much point in lingering—except I want a look at the muffling on the real sign." She crossed to it and played the beam of the torch over the dark material in which it was wrapped. "Noncommital—it's an old rubber sheet—but I think we'll take it along, as it may carry some clue. Also, removing it will lessen the chance of some other car's following the false directions."

"Hadn't you better drive on and let me stay and try to collar the brute when he comes to collect the substitute sign? He won't dare leave it in that position, for fear of useless accident."

"I'm not so sure of that—doubt if he'd risk being captured for the sake of saving innocent lives. He'll most likely stay in hiding until sure we've gone on, or else, if he's at all squeamish, got a bit down the road and stop anyone coming along."

She went slowly back to her car, carrying the rubber sheet which Calhoun had helped her to unfasten.

"For God's sake hurry!" He finally besought, unable to longer control his burning anxiety. "Ever since you suggested a possible watcher, I've been momentarily expecting to see you shot before my eyes!"

"Not a particle of danger." She so far humored him as to slip into her place behind the wheel. "Whoever planned my untimely death and intended it to look like an accident—they'd no intention of bringing the whole police force about their ears by openly murdering me. Don't you

realize that with the true sign once restored to its normal aspect and the false one removed, there'd have been
nothing to suggest foul-play? It would have looked like
something gone wrong with the steering gear, and the car
would probably have been too smashed up to tell tales."

"You're an amazing young person!" sincerely he informed her. "After escaping death by the narrowest of mar-
gins, you're as cool as an iced cucumber."

"Well, in one way the incident's a decided compliment
to my sleuthing ability. Somebody evidently thinks I'm
dangerous enough to be worth removing!"

"Any guess as to who that somebody is?"

"Not definitely—still, the field of suspects is a bit limited. I can only think of three people who, if they happen to be guilty of Leslie Carew's murder, have lately had
reason to think me hot on their trail. They are Rosamond
Forbes—the Queen of Hearts, whom we strongly suspect
of being Lydia Chadwick—and Inga Farrar."

"How about Truxton Manning?"

"He's out of it—the actual murder I mean—as reliable
witnesses swear he was in Chicago."

"He might have committed it by proxy."

"With what motive? No, I think he's hardly the type to
employ a hired assassin. If there was any killing to be done
he'd attend to it himself—though I imagine it would have
to be done in the heat of some violent passion. Don't lose
sight of the fact that, so far as we know, he'd no earthly
reason to desire Leslie's death. The only people with real
reasons for wanting her out of the way are: Mrs. Sarah
Carew, to retain her grandson—Lydia Chadwick, to inher-
it that thirty thousand, which she daren't claim at present,
by the way—and Inga Farrar, to prevent her marriage with
the man whom Inga herself seems to almost worship."

"Putting up the fake sign could hardly be the work of a
woman," Calhoun pointed out.

"Of course not. It's reasonable to suppose some man, tool or accomplice, watched to see what way we were taking, passed us on the road and arranged things for our reception."

"The motorcyclist who rode by at such a thundering pace!"

"Exactly."

12

The Second Murder

"Of all the foolhardy proceedings—your coming back to the Fifty-Three Limited, after what happened last night, is the worst!"

Calhoun fairly glared across the table at Tam, who answered his worried look with her sweetest smile.

"Not at all! Aren't all our pet suspects here—even Rosamond? And only think how annoyed someone must be, because I'm still in the land of the living!"

"Well, that's nothing short of a miracle, considering the chances you take," he grumbled. "If you'd only give up this hair-raising profession of yours, and consent to live a normal feminine life—"

"And leave poor Dad in the lurch with nothing to amuse his old age? I'm surprised at you, advising such selfishness!"

"Don't pretend it's anything but love of the work itself that keeps you in it!"

"As far as that goes, what safer love could a woman have? True, I may some day be successfully shuffled off this mortal coil; but at least I run no danger of heartbreak, which, I fancy, is sometimes harder to bear than a short sharp end."

"You're impossible!"

"So I've been told by others of your sex," she responded meekly. "But I've never at all agreed with them—I insist on considering my present mode of life very much worth while. Now, getting back to a really interesting subject, I learned today that Inga Farrar was absent from the *Flaming Tropics* cast on the night of Leslie's death—she sent word to her manager that she was suddenly ill and her understudy would have to appear in her stead."

"Phew!" He gave vent to a long, muted whistle. "Looks as if Jones' mysterious lady with the pistol may have really been Inga Farrar!"

"Yet, if so, how did she get away from Meadow Dale? Suppose Jones actually drove her to the club grounds—no one saw her leave them. There's not been the faintest hint of any veiled stranger seen on a road, or at the station. And while we're speaking of getaways, how did Lydia Chadwick, supposing her to have been Leslie's supper guest, manage to both reach and leave the club without being seen by anyone who recognized her? There must have been a number of Lydia's old friends and acquaintances among the club guests and attendants, and you know what long memories country people have."

"You love piling up difficulties, don't you?"

"Just as well to notice they're there—otherwise they've a nasty habit of cropping up at the eleventh hour and smashing one's most cherished theories. By the way, you mentioned knowing Leslie at the time of her marriage; didn't you know Lydia as well?"

"No, she'd already dropped out of the picture. I only met Leslie after she became engaged to my best friend, Eric Carew."

Just then their coffee was served, black and fragrant, and Tam's perfectly cut nose wrinkled ever so delicately with the appreciation of the admitted coffee lover. But she was fated never to enjoy that particular demi-tasse; a

waiter hurried to inform her in a confidential whisper that
she was wanted on the phone by "long distance!" Tam was
immediately intrigued; it flashed across her mind that no
one except Calhoun himself had known she was to be at
this night club; someone must have been on watch, perhaps have phoned out to a confederate. In any case, the
thing to do was to ascertain who was calling her. She left
Calhoun at the table, and went down to the telephone
booths on the lower floor.

There the operator directed her to of the closed booths,
where she sent answered "hello's" over an apparently open
wire until a bored, voice finally quired: "What number,
please?" Realizing that the connection must have been cut,
Tam appealed first to central, then to long distance, finally
to the switchboard operator, only to be told that the party
"must have hung up." There no long-distance record, that
was certain, so suspecting a stall, Tam sighed resignedly and
went back upstairs. Oakley Calhoun rose as she entered the
booth, and she saw that he had moved into her former seat.

"I shifted because Manning and Inga seemed to be having a row and I could watch them more easily from your
place. But I couldn't at all make out what it was about.
They've just patched up a peace and left, together, only an
instant ago."

The change of places seemed utterly unimportant and
Tam dropped into the chair his move had left vacant.

"I suppose the coffee's nearly stone cold. Shall we send
for some fresh?"

"Oh, it hasn't been standing so very long, probably it's
still decently hot." He dropped in three lumps of sugar,
stirred, then tasted it and added another.

"Heavens, do you always ruin your coffee by turning it
into a syrup?"

"Mere matter of taste. I like it well sweetened and this
particular brew is strong enough to walk alone."

He drank it, while Tam dropped in one conservative lump, then further delayed drinking in order to light a cigarette. She had taken no more than the initial puff when a queer, strangled sound from Calhoun made her look at him; to meet an expression in his staring black eyes which she would never be able to forget.

Slowly Calhoun's face went livid; his open mouth struggled to catch at the failing breath, then, like a blown-up manikin suddenly deflated, he collapsed across the table. Even before she touched him, Tam knew that he was dead.

So discreetly lighted was the booth, so almost noiseless the short, fatal scene, that the diners' first intimation that anything was wrong came when Tam's slender figure appeared at the booth entrance—her icily authoritative voice cutting across the hum of low-toned conversation: "There has been murder done here—anyone who leaves this room does so at the risk of drawing suspicion on themselves!"

She was alone, with no power to bar the various doors against their exit—Tam believed that only an appeal to their own self-interest could hold the crowd until the coming of the police.

"Murder!"

The word was tossed from table to table, but Tam had calculated correctly—such of the patrons as were not held by morbid curiosity remained because they feared laying themselves open to suspicion. She stood, alone but dominant.

The Joker had been absent from the room. But in some mysterious way the news of disaster instantly spread to the club's inner rooms and he appeared, white lipped and trembling, pushing a way through the crowd that had rapidly gathered around Tam, trying to peer over her shoulder at the sprawling figure across the table top. Tam firmly held the booth entrance, permitting no one to enter—not even the Joker himself.

"No. Nothing must be disturbed before the police arrive."

"The police—a murder—it means the club's ruin!" He despairingly wrung fat white hands, seemed to have lost all power of adequately meeting the emergency.

Tam, after one scornful glance, retained control. "Have your men guard all the exits. Let no one leave this room, or the house. And you, personally, phone police headquarters, instantly. Ask for Inspector Peter McCoy of the Homicide Bureau—if he's not there, try his home." She gave the number. "Hurry—I'll see that nothing's touched here."

As it happened, Inspector McCoy was at his home, at no great distance from the Fifty-Three Limited, so he was the first to arrive on the scene. At sight of Tam o' Shanter on guard at the stall entrance, he hurried across to her.

"Who is it?" McCoy had been told, over the phone, only that someone had been killed in the club's supper room.

"Oakley Calhoun—the man I brought to your office."

"How?"

"Poisoned coffee—I think it was meant for me, not for him."

The Inspector unceremoniously herded the curious supper crowd into the end of the room farthest from the booth where Calhoun's body lay. When comparative privacy was secured, he turned back to her. "Tell me what you know, before the medical examiner gets here."

"It's probably a sequel to the Carew murder on Long Island," she told him rapidly. "Of course I'm not certain, but the indications point that way. Oakley Calhoun was one of the two men who found the body in the country club summer house, and he's been working with me on the case ever since. Lately, as you already know, the trail has led here to the Fifty-Three Limited—I haven't time, now, to tell you exactly how and why, but we'll go into that later. Just now it's sufficient to say that a certain card, the Ace of Diamonds, appears to play an important role in the Carew murder. Of course not the actual card itself, but the club member known by that name. As a matter of fact, we've no definite knowledge of the Ace of Diamond's real identity as yet; but he, or she, thought we were closing in on them, and last night tried to summarily end my earthly activities."

She hastily sketched the episode of the false road sign, then went on:

"Mr. Calhoun begged me not to come here tonight. But I felt if the trail was getting hot enough to make such risky measures necessary, I couldn't afford to miss any chance of identifying the Ace by staying away. It never occurred to me that they'd venture on foul play here, in the midst of so many people—and— Oh, Mac! Instead of getting me, it's Calhoun they've killed! He was my friend—he—he— Oh, I'll never forgive myself!"

Her beautiful Irish voice quivered as McCoy had never heard it do before. His shrewd blue eyes watched her pityingly, while sympathy made his own voice unusually brusque.

"If you were together, how the deuce did they manage to poison either one of you, let alone the wrong one?"

"Just as our coffee was served, I went downstairs to answer a telephone call—obviously it was a fake message, intended to get me away while the poison was dropped into my coffee. How they contrived to get Calhoun to leave our table, I don't yet know."

"Sure it was the coffee?"

"Fairly sure. He died only a few seconds after drinking it—I hadn't tasted mine."

"Then, as far as you know, they may have intended getting you both?"

"Possibly, though I doubt it. My bet is, this other cup will analyze free of poison. They apparently had no grudge against Calhoun. Indeed, last night they went to some trouble to detain him in the city so he shouldn't be included in my scheduled smash-up."

"Then why doctor his cup, in place of yours?"

"They didn't! We accidentally changed places—a thing they couldn't have foreseen. When I came back from answering the phone, he'd shifted to my seat so as more easily to watch two of the people we've been interested in. It didn't seem to matter, so I took his chair. But don't forget, the coffee was already on the table when I left—either they lured him away and poisoned my cup while we were both absent, or else they poisoned it in the kitchen. They naturally couldn't know we'd shift as we did."

"Colossal nerve! Surely someone among all this crowd must have seen who went near your booth while you were absent."

"Not necessarily. You know who little the average person really sees. If the poisoner behaved in any unusual way, someone probably noticed; but if he, or she, just casually strolled into the booth and out again, as if having a perfect right there, it's a thousand to one nobody paid the slightest attention."

"Afraid you're right—the average citizen does go through the world with his faculty of observation carefully put away in cotton-wool," McCoy acknowledged. "Here are Dr. Hayden and a dozen men from headquarters."

The medical examiner, with Tam and McCoy, retired into the fatal booth, while the newly arrived detectives started rounding up the club members and guests, collecting their reluctantly-given names and addresses and warning them against attempting to leave before the preliminary examination of the body was finished and the Inspector found time to question them.

Calhoun's body was presently carried to an inner room where Dr. Hayden could more thoroughly examine it. The contents of Tam's coffee cup and the few drops remaining in Calhoun's were emptied into separate, carefully sealed bottles, to be later submitted for chemical analysis, and the fingerprint expert began an exhaustive search for enlightening prints, though little along that line could be hoped from a place normally frequented by so many different people.

The first preliminaries over, Inspector McCoy gathered all patrons and waiters who had been in the supper-room at the moment of Calhoun's sudden death, then informed them that, judging by the facts at present known, the police believed someone had introduced a deadly poison into the coffee of one of the diners during the few minutes while his booth was left empty.

"First of all, I want every one of you to concentrate on trying to remember anything that happened in or near the booth during the few minutes in question." Inspector McCoy's voice and manner, far from carrying the faintest taint of bullying took them all into his confidence, frankly asked their co-operation; and they responded by a loss of the sullenly resentful attitude which had hitherto characterized the large majority.

"Do any of you remember seeing Miss O'Brien, here, leave the booth?"

Two men did. A member and a waiter remembered seeing her pass through the room on her way downstairs.

"Now, which waiter was it who told her she was wanted on the phone?"

Nobody answered. If the desired waiter was still there, he refrained from proclaiming the fact. After a moment's wait McCoy went on to his next question.

"Anybody see Mr. Calhoun talking to anyone, man or woman, after Miss O'Brien went downstairs?"

Apparently no one had. McCoy grunted disgustedly, but held his usually peppery temper under firm curb; these people were not of a class from which the best results could be got by bullying.

"I realize there was nothing to make you specially notice Mr. Calhoun's actions—but didn't any of you happen to see him leave the booth?"

"Oh, yes, I saw him do that!" One of the women guests promptly volunteered. "You didn't put it like that before—you asked if we'd seen him talking to any one, and I hadn't."

McCoy turned his full attention on the speaker. "He left the booth, then?"

"Yes, sir."

"Alone?"

"Quite alone."

"Did he seem at all distressed or uneasy?"

"Not in the least. He simply strolled over to the alcove where cigars and cigarettes are sold, made some purchase, then went directly back to the booth."

"Then he did speak to someone—the cigar-stand attendant?"

"I suppose he must have done so," said the guest.

"Thank the Lord somebody in this crowd used their eyes!" was the inspector's fervent comment. "This young lady has explained his reason for leaving the table and pretty well established that he wasn't decoyed away, as we had thought. Can't someone else carry on the good work and tell us who entered the booth while Mr. Calhoun was buying a smoke?"

Nobody could, or at least nobody did, though the probabilities were strongly in favor of the poisoner's being among those who listened—unless— Tam, for the first time, recalled Calhoun's remark that Truxton Manning and Inga Farrar had left the supper room only an instant before her return. Could either of them be guilty?

One of the patrons with a deductive turn of mind here created a diversion by inquiring if the coffee might not have been poisoned before ever reaching the supper room.

"We can't tell that until the contents of both cups have been analyzed," McCoy patiently explained. "It was poured from a common coffee pot, so if the poison is confined to only one cup, it must have been put there after the liquid left the container in which it was originally brought to the table. Now, I'm going to give you all a few minutes in which to think back,—hope you'll try your darnedest to remember seeing someone near that booth—man, woman or child—not even waiters excepted."

The effort proved unavailing. In a crowded room, where a constant stream of people was passing in various directions, it was hardly surprising that the poisoner's movements should have so melted into the general scene as to escape notice. One old lady admitted a vague impression of having seen some woman hovering near the fatal booth; but she was so unsure of the time, or indeed of the woman's appearance at all, that her evidence failed to help.

After a few more unsuccessful attempts to elicit information, the Inspector gave it up and allowed them to disperse. Then followed a consultation with Dr. Hayden, who had by this time made as thorough an examination of the body as was possible under the given conditions.

"I'll perform an autopsy tomorrow," he promised, "in the hope of discovering precisely what poison was used. It seems to have been some intensely powerful drug, producing instant death by paralysis of respiration. I'd say it was cyanide."

"There's no possibility of natural death?"

"Certainly not! You can set your mind at rest on that score." The doctor departed, having first arranged for the removal of Calhoun's body, and a little later Tam suggested

adjournment to some place where she and Inspector Mc-
Coy could go over the case from its inception.

"Why not drive over to my home?" suggested Tam. "We
can talk there undisturbed and Hannah's so used to my
unholy hours that she won't mind giving us coffee, even if
it is close to morning."

"Better let our talk wait till tomorrow," McCoy demurred. "I ought to put in my report tonight."

"You can make it a much fuller one if you first let me
post you on the Carew case."

Which consideration induced him to postpone the
turning in of his report on Calhoun's death.

13

Three Women

Tam's quaint and at the same time extremely comfortable city home was the upper floor of a remodeled building which had once done duty as a wealthy man's stable. In its present renovated state it possessed but two tenants, old Herman Klotz, a dealer in antiques, and Tam o' Shanter herself. She had taken the place, in a quiet backwater of old New York, at the beginning of her career as professional investigator of crimes; and now, when many successful cases would have amply justified more expensive quarters, nothing short of fire or earthquake could have persuaded her to move.

Her small household, consisting of middle-aged Hannah, the housekeeper, and a boy just under twelve known as Dips, were so accustomed to her uncertain hours while she was actively engaged on a case, that neither evinced the slightest surprise when she and McCoy turned up in the middle of the night. Hannah promptly set about the preparing of coffee while Dips, still half asleep but mightily pleased by Tam's unexpected arrival, volunteered a report on his last night's shadowing of the blonde about whom she had telephoned.

"I told you to let me know if anything important resulted," Tam reminded him.

"Sure. But there wasn't nothin'—leastways, allowin' I followed the right dame. Did she have on a dress near the color o' orange jouice, and a fetthery sort of cape?"

"Yes."

"Must ha' been her, all right—washed-out lookin', same as ef the laundry used lye when she was done up. She didn't do nuthin', just took a taxi and I hooked on behind—druv to a West side apartment house; I got the number down. Went in like she belonged, and stayed there, never showed a nose again."

"A large apartment house?"

"Sure."

"You didn't happen to see any motorcycles near it?"

"No. What's the big idea?"

"Tell you later. Mac and I need a talk now."

As concisely as she could without losing sight of any apparently relevant detail, Tam gave him all her facts and suspicions touching the murder of young Mrs. Carew, and its sequel crime. Much of it was already known to him through printed accounts, but a good deal had been kept from the press and was consequently new.

"Odd case," he remarked thoughtfully when she had finished. "Seem to be only women concerned. As you tell it, a young social leader is found dead with the only people who've any reason to wish her out of the way all belonging to her own sex. Rosamond Forbes, mother-in-law, sister—and the unknown lady of the taxi.

"Four women, all with more or less strong motives for removing her. Up to date there doesn't seem so much as one suspicious male anywhere in the offing."

"I think Oakley Calhoun's death completely clears Mrs. Sarah Carew," Tam cut in. "So far as we know, she couldn't have considered herself threatened by our interest in the Fifty-Three Limited. She had no reason for trying to eliminate me at that place—and apparently no contact with it at all."

"But of the three suspects left, we're uncertain how close they are to the club. Take the Forbes woman first. She's a member—think she had any reason to believe you were closing in on her?"

"No I don't. She'd be more apt to believe my interest in the club was due to the hunt for Lydia Chadwick."

"Feel certain that's the Queen of Heart's real name?"

"Nearly. Don't you agree?"

"Too new on the case for definite opinions." McCoy hedged. "I'd like knowing more about this Ace of Diamonds—she hooks closest with the death-weapon."

"Already decided the Ace is a woman?"

"Haven't we concluded this is an all-woman case, no men suspects allowed? What bothers me most is the summer house—why was the body tricked out like that? And how did whoever arranged it lay hands on so many articles at short notice? Gives a hint of premeditation."

Tam's smoothly cropped dark head gestured a negation. "There was nothing that couldn't have been picked up at, or near the scene," she informed him. "The iridescent gauze was part of Leslie's own evening dress. The deck of cards matched those stocked by the Country Club for the use of its members. The poinsettia flower and wine glass probably came from room 14, likewise the sugar. The candle sticks were also the club's property, while the pillows were already in the summer house, having been used there during the afternoon. The only thing that required special preparation was the oblong of white wrapping paper bearing a string of printed numbers, and even that was roughly executed—it wouldn't have taken long to make."

"Queer, that last. You've not even a guess as to why that list of numbers was tucked under her feet?"

"No. The brute of a thing has haunted me from the beginning! Just about sat on my pillow edge and kept me awake, but I can't make it mean a thing."

"Still, it must have been put there for some reason." The inspector pointed out.

"Don't you suppose I realize that? The best I can offer is that the numbers held some special significance for both the dead woman and her murderer—but I'm completely in the dark as to what that significance could have been."

"They say the more bizarre features surround a crime, the easier it is to solve," McCoy discontentedly complained. "This case seems an exception—all that fancy stage setting has led nowhere at all."

"Wrong, old dear—it's at least furnished some enlightening hints. Take the candles for instance. By testing identical ones belonging to the club, Calhoun and I were able to pretty closely determine how long they'd been burning when found."

"Motiveless sort of thing—setting so many alight to advertise the crime!"

"How can we tell?" she argued. "There may have been some reason why it fitted the murderer's plan to have Leslie's body found at a given hour."

"Taken by and large, it's the Devil's own case!" McCoy gave as his opinion after a meditative pause. "Thankful to say it's yours, not mine. My responsibility begins and ends with the murder of Oakley Calhoun."

"So you don't think the two crimes are connected?"

"It's too early to say, one way or the other. Tell me: Have you any idea at all who killed the woman?"

"A very strong idea, Mac. But as you've so often told me yourself, I'm waiting till I get a few missing links that will clinch the case.

McCoy shot her a keen look, then held out an empty coffee cup. As Tam replenished it from the tray which Hannah had placed beside her during the initial stages of their talk, Dips for the first time asked a question.

"Wasn't nothin' seen of the dame's other clothes—not nothin' at all?"

"No, Dips. The State Police searched every conceivable place—even offered a reward to anyone giving information that would lead to their recovery, but nothing happened."

"Suppose a few underthings wouldn't make much of a bundle," McCoy reflected aloud, "even with slippers and stockings added. All the same, with the eyes of the whole countryside sharpened by thoughts of that reward, it's strange nothing was found. Get a description of the outfit?"

"Of course, from Mrs. Sarah Carew, later supplemented by the lady's maid. She wore a rather long, straight cut underdress, made of silvery cloth brocaded with a design of water lilies in the palest shell pink—over which the yards of gauze enwrapping Leslie's body were originally draped so as to form the irregular hemline that's so effective in a frock meant for dancing."

"Jumping Saint Peter! I didn't ask for a catalogue description." McCoy remonstrated. "Only wanted an idea of how small the thing could be folded."

"Oh, small enough to form an unobtrusive package, I suppose, in case the murderer wanted to carry it away. But I've wondered if the clothes weren't simply tied around a rock and thrown into the Sound."

"Likely enough." The Inspector admitted. "Did you keep an eye out for them while hunting the pistol?"

"Yes, but the clothes would be harder to see because of their less definite outline. Once darkened by a thorough soaking, they'd be apt to blend in with seaweed and stray stones. Anyway, I never could find them, though I searched several times."

"Better forget them for the time being," McCoy advised. "We've got to concentrate on the Fifty-Three Limited and who doctored that coffee. As early as I decently can, I'll get the Joker, as they call Davis, down to headquarters and grill him into telling us who's known as the Ace of Diamonds. That ought to give us a lead where to start."

"Why us? A moment ago you disclaimed all responsibility in the Carew case."

"Oh well, we've so often worked together it's a bit of a habit—besides, you're probably right in thinking only Leslie Carew's murderer had a motive for wanting you removed at exactly this time. There's not much doubt the poison was really meant for you."

"I ought to have foreseen the danger, instead of blindly letting it overtake my friend." Tam sorrowfully reproached herself.

"No good thinking of that now! Better concentrate on trying to catch the party that killed him."

"I know, but that can't give him back the life of which my carelessness robbed him." Then, resolutely pushing aside regrets for her lost friend, Tam went on. "Mac, in the desire to cover everything, there's one clue I may have left unstressed. Whoever killed Leslie Carew knew her as a drug addict—that is, if the granulated sugar sprinkled under her body was put there for the reason we suppose."

"This coroner fellow admits she must have been taking hypodermic injections for some time?"

"Yes, but apparently she never became an absolute slave to the habit—probably had too strong a will, or too many other modes of making life exciting. Along that line of inquiry the main questions are: How many people knew she used morphine? And who were they?"

"May take a bit of time to answer them but it ought not to be very difficult; boils down to a process of elimination. We seem to be more or less running up against drugs in this inquiry—first Lydia Chadwick and her husband, later her sister. Think the Fifty-Three Limited is a drug distributing center?"

The question brought Tam squarely against a difficulty which she had clearly foreseen, but had not had time to consider. How much concerning the black and white booths had she the right to tell McCoy, in face of her own and Calhoun's pledge of secrecy, given in order to first gain admission to the club? They had promised the Joker to make no report at headquarters as to how it was run— in exactly what degree, if any, did Calhoun's death lessen her obligation to keep that promise? Unable to instantly decide, she busied herself with coffee and sandwiches to gain time for considering it, and in the end was saved the necessity of decision by McCoy's bringing up another subject.

"That confounded piece of numbered wrapping paper seems to be haunting me as you say it has you. Can't seem to get it out of my head. Suppose you couldn't draw me a picture of it from memory?"

"Easily."

She crossed to the desk and after a little search found an extra-large sheet on which she carefully printed the well-remembered numbers: "997033," using the butt-end of a match dipped in ink.

"Was that the method used in the original?" McCoy inquired, watching her.

"I think so, though it may have been done with a small brush."

He regarded the finished product with a puzzled scowl. "Evidently not a sum of money; there's no division between the figures. What the devil can it mean?"

"I'm rather beginning to fear we shan't know that, until the whole mystery's cleared up." Tam sounded a trifle discouraged, she hated being completely baffled in the effort to read some significance into a clue which, she felt, must hold an essential secret.

"Speaking of clearing up—do we work separately or together?" the Inspector asked.

"Which you like. Suppose we let our plan of action lie fallow till you've dragged the Ace of Diamonds' identity out of the Joker?"

They decided to let it temporarily rest at that, and snatch a few hours sleep. But after he had gone and her small household returned to their beds, Tam found the oblivion of sleep quite unattainable. She had not previously realized the depths of her very genuine liking for Oakley Calhoun, and his sudden death had shaken her beyond reach of her usually sane acceptance of Life's accomplished tragedies—the more so, because she felt herself in a certain sense to blame. If she had only not insisted on a return to the night club after once realizing the desperate lengths to which her antagonists were prepared to go!

Of course, Mac was right. There was no sense in brooding over Calhoun's loss. Yet she was unable to curb or control her insistent self reproach.

For a long time she stared, half unseeingly, at the printed oblong; "997083"—what did those six cryptic figures signify? No flash of intuition enlightened her and she finally put the sheet carefully away in the desk.

As she did so, the box from which she had taken the match used for printing it, fell to the floor. Stooping to retrieve it, she suddenly remembered the box of white-headed matches which Calhoun had shown her, on their last ride back to Meadow Dale.

What had become of them? She remembered his taking them from an outer coat pocket, but had failed to notice if they were afterward restored to the same resting place. At least he had neglected giving them to her, and she wondered if the police would find them on his body.

Well, if they did, the matches would tell their own tale; and once they were successfully linked with the Fifty-Three Limited, she would be relieved of her problem of deciding how much of the club's drug activities she had a right to tell. She lighted a cigarette and, feeling that going to bed would simply mean lying awake a helpless prey to remorseful thoughts, she gave herself over to concentrated study of the case.

14

A Passion Re-Born

Next morning the investigation suffered an unlooked-for check when the Joker, even under the most grilling questioning, maintained his entire ignorance of the Ace of Diamond's identity.

According to his story, the former wearer of the name had died about three months before and, perhaps six weeks afterward, the name had been assigned to some person still on the waiting list. But—and here came the catch which might or might not be true—the small committee in whose charge rested the admission of any chosen member to enrollment among the Fifty-Three, had neglected to pass on the favored name. The Joker stubbornly insisted that he had no idea who had been given the Ace of Diamonds title, and furthermore declared it would be impossible to learn the new user's identity without a delay of some few days, as all five members of the electing committee happened to be out of town.

Much annoyed by the unforeseen check, McCoy sent some of his men to look up the members of the electing committee within easiest reach. He gave most of his own day to preliminary spade-work, such as questioning various witnesses more closely, investigating the scene of Calhoun's death and studying the medical examiner's report.

Part of the time Tam o' Shanter worked with him, but she seemed to be nursing some private plan of her own, in which she showed no inclination to include him, and he retaliated by following the Queen of Heart's spoor without her assistance.

At the apartment address furnished by Dips, Inspector McCoy unearthed anything but satisfactory information. He learned that a Mr. and Mrs. Wickman had occupied a furnished apartment them for some time past, but the night of Calhoun's death they had unceremoniously departed, leaving a portion of the rent unpaid, but carefully taking all their personal possessions with them. No one seemed to know at exactly what hour the exit had been accomplished. A search of the deserted apartment yielded very little; there was nothing to show whither they had flitted. The Inspector's only real satisfaction came with the discovery of an overlooked cache of heroin accidentally left behind.

Altogether the case was progressing in a most unsatisfactory manner, and after dinner McCoy rang Tam up with the idea of friendly consultation, only to learn that she was out and had left no word as to when she might be expected to return, He rang headquarters and the Fifty-Three Limited, then, hearing nothing of Tam at either place, gave it up and morosely retired into study of his copious notes on the perplexing case.

Meanwhile, Tam was serenely enjoying a most excellent dinner at a restaurant chosen because it was a favorite with Inga Farrar; a fact ascertained through inquiry among some former members of *The Flaming Tropics* cast. Tam feared that an open visit to the dancer would prove fruitless; Inga would most probably refuse to receive her. So she planned a surprise campaign.

Luck was with her, for Inga presently entered the cafe with two women friends, and through generous bribing of the waiter who served them, Tam learned that while the two friends intended to go on to a show, Inga herself planned an immediate return to her apartment, the address of which Tam already knew from the telephone directory.

She paid her own dinner check and slipped out through a side entrance, taking a taxi across town; so that when Inga Farrar entered the lobby of her expensive apartment house home, she found Tam quietly waiting for her. There was no way of shaking Tam off without an actual scene, for Tam quite obviously had no intention of being evaded, so Inga succumbed to the unavoidable with a fairly good grace. The two women went up to Inga's floor together.

Outside her own door Inga paused, key in hand, to regard her unwelcome visitor with openly hostile eyes.

"What do you want with me, anyway?" she demanded. "Think I'm mixed up with the Carew murder?"

"I haven't suggested such a thing," Tam serenely responded. "Why jump at unpleasant conclusions?"

"Truxton told me I'd been a fool to talk so frankly in the dressing room! Now I suppose you'll make me doubly sorry. Well, come on in—I can't leave you outside without risking a lot of publicity I can't afford."

"Just a second."

As Inga reached out to insert her key, an opal bracelet which she wore came full into the overhead light and Tam saw its pattern—a lace-like scroll, each group of small, platinum-set flower sprays radiating from one of the large opals.

It was an uncommon design, and as Tam looked at it, she entertained not a particle of doubt that the delicate diamond spray found near the scene of Leslie Carew's murder had been broken from this identical bracelet.

So—another clue strongly pointing to Inga Farrar's presence close to the summer house on the night of Leslie's death! Still, this was not the moment to put Inga further on guard by questions, so Tam hid her interest in the bracelet and let the dancer open her door.

The large room into which it gave was in darkness until Inga switched on the light, and, moving with her usual rapidity, crossed it to fling up the blind of a closed window, meaning to open it. As the blind whirred up, both women caught an instantaneous glimpse of a man standing on the fire escape—his ear pressed against the window crack.

Then he took a startled backward step, lost his footing and disappeared into space.

For a second neither moved or spoke. Then Inga clutched her throat with a strangled cry:

"My God—he's fallen!— And we're eleven flights up!"

Tam failed to answer in words. Instead she pushed up the window, leaning out into the light-sprinkled darkness.

Through the bottom slats of the fire escape she could see that there was no unusual crowd on the sidewalk beneath it, as would surely have been the case had a man suddenly plunged to his death there.

"I think he's fallen down the fire-escape stairs!" She turned to the distracted Inga. "Shall we give the alarm or go down ourselves?"

Without waiting for an answer, Tam slipped through the window and started down the iron stairs. At their foot a man lay huddled, apparently unconscious.

"Have you a match?" Tam called to Inga, who had followed and was close behind.

Inga hadn't; like Tam herself, she had dropped her purse before venturing onto the fire-escape. While Inga ran back up the stairs, Tam knelt, running skilled fingers over the motionless figure on the landing—his heart beat steadily, and she believed him no more than stunned. A moment later Inga returned, leaning over her shoulder as she struck a match, so that its light might fall directly on the unconscious man. As it did so, a piercing cry broke from her startled lips— It was Truxton Manning.

"Hush!" Tam cautioned. "We don't want the whole apartment house about our ears!"

A downward glance showed her that one or two passers-by had paused and were looking up, attracted by the dancer's frantic scream. Then, as no sound followed it and the crouching figures on the landing were too high up to be easily seen against the dark bulk of the wall, they went on.

"I think he's coming to. Take hold of his shoulder so he can't thrash around and perhaps fall further down."

Inga mutely did as she was told so that when Manning opened dazed eyes he found himself firmly grasped by two business-like pairs of hands.

"No use struggling, Mr. Manning!" Tam warned him as he instinctively tried to throw them off. "You've been caught in the act and may as well come back upstairs and give an account of yourself—that is, if you can manage the climb."

"Inga?"

"I'm here," she answered. Something in her tone, vibrant, almost menacing, made Tam glance at her doubtfully. Nor did Inga offer the slightest help in the difficult climb up the stairs; it was Tam's shoulder that did duty as a crutch.

Once safe in Inga's room Manning sank onto a lounge and very nearly lapsed back into unconsciousness—it was only Inga's voice, low pitched but furious, that cut through the gathering obscurity and brought him to sharp realization of the moment.

"How do you dare spy on me, Truxton Manning?" She fairly hissed at him. "Even if I'd taken another lover, had you the right to object? Wasn't it you that threw away all claim to my love?"

"It wasn't that," Manning weakly protested. "I wanted to be sure—"

The unknown intruder took a startled step backward—
then lost his balance and toppled off the fire escape

"Sure that I was alone, still mourning you!" She interrupted. "Have I ever given you anything but the truth?
Why weren't you man enough to ask if I'd replaced you—
instead of sneaking, spying—"

"Be quiet!" he ordered, his voice filled with anger as
hot as her own. "I had to be sure, not if you'd taken a lover—but if you'd killed Leslie Carew!"

"You thought that!"

"How could I not think it?— I knew your pistol!"

"Ah!" It was a soft moan of unbearable pain—pain that
seemed to wipe out all Inga's former rage. "So it was to trap
me you came to the theater—and I, poor fool, dreamed it
was some shred of your old affection that made you turn
to me for comfort!"

"Wait—" He raised on one elbow, staring at her with an
expression compounded of several conflicting emotions.
Both of them had completely forgotten Tam's presence and
she took care not to in any way remind them. "At the inquest I saw your pistol—the one from Italy, I'd given you
myself, years ago—produced as the murder-weapon. I saw
the flower-spray broken from your bracelet!— Naturally I
thought you'd read of our engagement, tried to make her
give me up—"

"I did just that!" Inga broke in before he could finish.
"The Sunday paper told me you planned marrying her, and
I couldn't bear it—I found she was to be at the Country
Club dance, where I could quite easily get at her, so I went
there meaning to force her into breaking the engagement.
I hid in the shrubbery and watched—the paper had print-
ed her picture, several of them; I felt I'd know that woman
at sight.

"By and by she came out of the club, alone and strolled
off into the grounds. I followed till she was close to that
summer house, a long way from other people. Then I
stopped her—told her what you'd been to me, said that I'd

sooner kill than let her have you. She wasn't frightened—if she had been it might have ended differently—but she was only interested and rather pleased—she thanked me for giving her such a marvelous thrill! And then she laughed at me, saying no man was worth such senseless devotion, that I'd be wiser to forget you as you'd already forgotten me. The world was full of other men, why not use my beauty to ensnare some fresher love? Why waste it in vain pining for you?

"I tried to stop her—threatened to shoot if she didn't promise to give you up—but she only laughed and laughed—I couldn't do it, couldn't give her the death she seemed not to fear at all! I was ashamed of my own cowardice, ashamed that I couldn't silence her mockery—so—I—dropped the pistol and fled."

"Is that the truth?" The oil man questioned almost savagely. "Are you innocent of her murder?"

"Still bent on trapping me?" She sneered at him. "On exacting blood-vengeance for her spilled blood?"

"God! I wasn't trying to trap, but to protect you! When I saw that pistol, and thought you'd killed her, I learned what you meant to me—learned that regardless of what you'd done, you were still my woman—it was up to me to save you! That's why I had to be sure, had to know just what I was up against—"

"You meant protecting me, even if I'd killed the woman you loved?" Inga's tone held open incredulity.

"Sudden death opens one's eyes. He retorted with a certain grimness. "I found it was mostly the glamor of her social position, her dainty worldliness, that had enthralled me—put to the test my real love was yours."

With a soft little cry of sheer rapture, Inga rushed across to crouch at his side, face buried against his body.

"No need to take it so hard." Manning laughed a bit shakily, while one big hand stroked the bowed, black head.

"After all, we're two of a kind, you and I, neither of us meant for the smooth-surfaced life of the socially elite. We've been used to battling against odds all our lives, and the process has deepened our lusts and our loves—insipid ease couldn't hold much lasting charm. So—when I thought you guilty of murder, I kept you under my eyes, watched to see if the police were closing in. Sudden flight would have called their attention, even if they hadn't previously suspected you; but I arranged for a rapid get-a-way in case of need. A friend I can trust has chartered a yacht in his own name—it's ready to put to sea at a moment's notice. But first I wanted to be sure if you were really guilty. Not that it mattered— I only wanted to know."

Suddenly a look of chill horror spread over the man's dark, intent face; he had remembered Tam's presence. Very slowly he turned to stare at her, mingled rage and entreaty in his eyes.

"God, I've shown you my hand— What's the next move?"

"Nothing worse than a few explanations." Tam told him with a disarming

smile. "You see, I believe Inga's telling the truth!"

"So do I! But that's mainly what you might term my conceit—I doubt if anything could induce her to lie to me. All the same, facts are damnably against her; there's no real reason for you to think her innocent."

"My impression's the same as yours—you'd both forgotten I was here, and she spoke for your benefit, not mine. Also, intense anger is a great truth-breeder; if she'd really shot Leslie, I don't for a moment believe she'd have denied the fact."

"You're right, she was mad enough to have thrown it in my teeth—she has hell's own temper once it's roused, has this woman of mine."

Again his strong hand caressed the head pressed so closely against him, and Inga caught it in both of hers, to press passionate kisses on his open palm. At the touch of her lips, Manning's face softened unbelievably. He looked down at her, then lifted his anxious eyes to Tam.

"What had we better do?" There was an almost boyish pleading in his usually authoritative voice.

"First of all, I'll need to ask you both some questions." She settled into a nearby, chair and reached for a cigarette. "Inga is the Ace of Diamonds?"

He merely nodded, and she promptly added a second question. "According to the Joker's story, she was only assigned that title a few weeks ago. How does her pistol happen to carry the same emblem? Was it put there after her election?"

"No, it was originally one of a set of four that I bought in Italy—the others had an inlaid spade, club, and heart. Inga preferred the diamond, and I gave it to her years ago. I think the others are still in my California home."

"So her being given the same club-card was only a co-incidence?"

"As to that, I can't say. After we broke off our affair, I never saw Inga until Leslie was dead. I can't help you about anything that happened in between." He touched the dancer's shoulder. "Sit up, girl, and help plan our campaign."

Inga obediently lifted a face transformed by happiness until its beauty almost startled Tam. She had evidently listened to their talk, for her first words answered the detective's question:

"It wasn't exactly coincidence. For some reason I was popular at the Fifty-Three Limited—most of the members I knew seemed to like me—so when I especially asked to be given the Ace of Diamonds title, both because of the pistol I often carried at night and because I'd several times worn that costume at masquerades, they agreed to let me have it."

"I only asked because I don't much trust coincidence," Tam explained. "There's generally something behind it. Did you know you'd lost that spray from your bracelet?"

"Yes, but I'd no idea where; the papers never mentioned its having been found in Meadow Lane."

"That was one of the things we kept from the reporters. The first time I saw you, the printed accounts of the murder seemed to be absorbing your attention to the exclusion of everything else."

"Well, how would you feel if you read that your own pistol had been found on the scene of a murder which only cowardice had prevented your really committing? It made me wonder if I hadn't suffered some strange amnesia and if the guilt wasn't really mine!"

"You actually doubted?"

"A little—until I realized that the weird treatment accorded the body couldn't have been my work. First, because the whole conception was unlike anything I'd ever have thought of; and second, because I was a stranger at the country club. I wouldn't have known where to find all the things used, and couldn't have got at them if I had known."

The same thought had already occurred to Tam. She nodded.

"You went out to Meadow Dale on a train reaching there at 9:28, didn't you? And took a taxi from the station to the club grounds?"

"Yes."

"Mind telling me how you managed to completely disappear after you'd seen Leslie Carew?"

"Why—it sounds rather stupid, but I simply walked and walked. I was so disgusted at my own weakness, and the way I'd run away from her taunts, that I had to work it out of my system by violent exercise. When I'd walked some seven or eight miles, I calmed down and began to think about getting back to the city. An obliging country-man directed me to the nearest railway station and I caught a late train. It was pure chance no one happened to see or remember me. After I left the club, I took no precautions as I'd no reason to guess there'd be any fatal aftermath to my scene with Mrs. Carew."

Tam carefully considered the story while they both watched her, apparently ready to resign the leadership into her more experienced hands.

"If you've given the details quite accurately, someone must have afterwards found the pistol you dropped—and used it. Any idea as to the exact time of your, we might as well call it, flight?"

"It's hard to say—the last time I looked at my watch was just before she came out of the club. It was then twenty-three minutes to eleven—walking to the summer house would take, how long?"

"From four to six minutes, according to the pace." Tam had timed the distance. "That takes us to seventeen min-utes before eleven at the latest. I suppose your quarrel, while violent, wasn't very prolonged?"

"How can I tell? It seemed as if she laughed and jeered for hours—but I suppose ten minutes may have been near-er the actual time."

"And Dr. Ramsey thinks she was shot close to eleven. That doesn't give much leeway; it suggests that the real murderer was there when you left. You didn't see or hear any concealed third, at your little interview?"

"No, but that doesn't prove there was no one there! I was much too engrossed in Leslie Carew to have noticed."

"If I'm to help you out of the mess you're in, you'll have to be perfectly frank," Tam warned. "And please remember —once the police know you're the Ace of Diamonds and that pistol belongs to you, it will be hard work convincing them you didn't use it."

"Do you suppose I haven't realized that? I've lived with the fear of a clutch on my shoulder ever since I read the pistol was found!"

"Then—straight truth, remember—did you think I was hot on your trail?"

"No! Sometimes I feared you might be, but I watched and thought you were more interested in Rosamond Forbes and the Queen of Hearts."

"Is the Queen really Leslie's sister, Lydia Chadwick?"

"Why, I don't know!" Inga's tone bespoke genuine surprise. "I never heard her real name and I don't know her at all well. While she's one of the original members, or so I've been told, she'd dropped out when I first joined the club and I only met her quite recently."

"How recently?"

Inga gravely considered the question before answering it. "I think, indeed I'm almost sure, it was the night after Leslie Carew's death."

"Oh." Tam nodded as if the date fitted some private theory of her own. "So she hadn't been frequenting the Fifty-Three Limited for some time? Ever see her husband?"

"I didn't even know she had one."

"He's not much of a specimen, but she may still be fond of him—there's no accounting for tastes. You know Rosamond Forbes more intimately?"

"Much; and I also know she's an old and close friend of the Queen of Hearts."

"Now, Mr. Manning, it's your turn to answer a question. What did you hand Rosamond Forbes in The Willows' garden, just as I arrived on the scene?"

"You've sharp eyes! I imagined you too far away to catch that little transaction. Since you weren't, I may as well confess making Rosamond a little cash present—just to ensure her keeping a still tongue about Inga's ownership of the death-pistol."

"Not blackmail?"

"Not in so many words. But the idea worked the same—her conscience required salving; it was troubling her because she hadn't told Ramsey she knew the gun's owner."

"Truxton—" Inga's tone was awed. "You were protecting me, then, right at the start?"

"I told you Leslie's death cleared my vision in several directions!" he told her almost curtly. "We'll indulge in sentiment just a bit later on—the thing at present is to decide our best course of action. Do you advise using that yacht, Miss O'Brien?"

"Heavens, no! It would look exactly like a confession, and probably wouldn't do the least good—you'd be traced by wireless. Much better face the situation. I'm afraid I can't keep you altogether out of trouble; it's an open question if Inspector McCoy will take my word for Inga's innocence, but I think he'll at least delay any arrest until some other lines of the investigation have been thoroughly worked. Do either of you know any facts about the Fifty-Three Limited's drug activities?"

"Speaking personally, I only know the stuff's to be had there," Manning answered. "Never using anything of the kind, I wasn't greatly interested."

"It was Leslie who first took you to the club?"

"Wrong; she never so much as mentioned the place. I was astonished when Inga took me there and several of the people I met spoke of Leslie's having frequented it."

"So—did you never suspect her as a morphine addict?"

"Never!" There was no doubting the reality of his amazement.

Tam sighed. "It would have made things easier if you two had been more on the inside. As you weren't, I'll have to get certain needed information elsewhere. Now for the present, just sit tight, both of you; I'll keep you posted on developments."

15
Peach-Colored Undergarments

The Queen of Hearts, otherwise known as Mrs. Wickman of the apartment house, and strongly suspected of being Lydia Chadwick, had succeeded in vanishing into thin air. Inspector McCoy's most strenuous efforts failed to unearth a single clue as to her whereabouts. And the more elusive she proved, the more convinced he became of her responsibility for Oakley Calhoun's murder.

He had not yet secured the electing committee's report on the Ace of Diamonds' identity, so he was feeling only a secondary interest in Inga Farrar—an interest Tam did nothing to augment during a lengthy conference, held the next morning at the Fifty-Three Limited.

So far, Inspector McCoy had picked up no hint of the club's being a narcotic station. And the fact caused Tam acute distress; she longed to warn him, but was doubtful in what degree their mutual pledge to the Joker bound her to silence. The ethical question was made the more difficult because she possessed no real proof that the said activities had had any direct connection with Calhoun's murder.

While with McCoy in the club supper room, she quietly examined the match boxes supplied in the black and white booths. Quite as she expected, they were now both furnished with perfectly innocent red-headed matches of

a well-known brand. Feeling that if she decided in favor
of frank speaking the cocaine-headed matches taken from
their stall on the night before Calhoun's death would be
needed to prove her accusation against the club, she simply told McCoy that she was driving out to Meadow Dale,
then phoned Owen Fitzharris to ask if he would help her
search Oakley Calhoun's possessions in quest of a mislaid clue. When his affirmative answer came back over the
wire, she set a time for her arrival at his cottage. Then she
paid a visit to Inga Farrar.

She found the dancer in a mood which Tam considered,
under the circumstances, almost idiotically blissful. The
fact that Inga had regained Truxton Manning's love, or
perhaps more accurately had never really lost it, appeared
to far outbalance her fear of possible arrest.

"Much good it will do you, once you're in jail," Tam
unfeelingly pointed out. "Can't you let sentiment wait
over until the case is cleared up?"

"Of course, only—it's so difficult to think of anything
else!" Inga joyously apologized. "Do you realize, he meant
saving me even if I'd really killed her?"

"Quite. I heard all about that last night—now it would
be a lot more helpful if you'd try to remember everything
you possibly can about the Queen of Hearts."

"As I told you, she only started coming to the club
quite lately and almost at once Truxton looked me up at
the theatre; he seemed to really like being

with me, so naturally I had no eyes for anyone else."

"A disease your tongue seems to have caught," Tam disgustedly complained. "Can't you even think about anything but that man?"

"I suppose you can't understand—you're not in love!"

"No, and may Heaven save me from ever falling into
that sublimely idiotic state!" Tam laughed. "You're utterly
hopeless!"

She gave up any attempt to pin Inga to mundane matters until her first ecstasy should subside, and started for her visit to Owen Fitzharris. He was interestedly awaiting her arrival, and at once led the way into the comfortable cottage sitting room.

"All Oakley's things are still here. In fact, I've no idea where to send them—as far as I know he hadn't a relation in the world."

"Yet you were close friends, weren't you?"

"Yes and no. That is, we've known each other for years, almost since we were boys in fact; but there've been long intervals during which we lost touch. I'd neither seen nor heard from him for a good three years before he turned up this summer."

"Was that before you came out to Meadow Dale?"

"No. I'd already taken on this cottage. Oakley and I met accidentally in a club we both belonged to. He was a bit at loose end, and so I asked him out to stop with me. Sorry enough I am!" He added regretfully. "If he'd stayed in town, he'd never have got involved in Mrs. Carew's murder and he would be still alive."

"You've not half the cause to regret your action that I have," Tam earnestly reminded him. "How much did he tell you of our joint discoveries?"

"Very little. I only know you were interested in some night club representing a deck of playing cards. Has the clue that's got itself mislaid any connection?"

"The closest. In fact, it's a box of white-headed matches, coming from said club. I'll tell you more about them later."

Oakley Calhoun had occupied a big, dormer-windowed bedroom on the upper floor of the tiny cottage, where his clothes and baggage, some of it still unpacked, remained exactly as he had left them.

First of all, Tam hunted through the pockets of the light overcoat he had worn over his evening clothes on the

night he acquired the white-headed matches. They were
not to be so easily found however nor did a minute search
through his more accessible belongings prove successful.

"Where *can* he have put them?" She finally demanded of Fitzharris. "They weren't on him at the time of his
death, otherwise the police would have found them; and
they didn't."

"Must have tucked them away so our maid wouldn't
accidentally interfere with them." He gazed rather helplessly about the room. "Would he lock them up in a suit-
case, do you think?"

"Hard to tell. I suppose we'll have to go through his
luggage if we can't find them outside it. What's in that low
cupboard under the eaves?"

"Mostly trash, I think. I remember once seeing him
stick some crab nets in there. Let's have a look."

Tam knelt before the little cupboard and opened its
door; the just mentioned crab-nets were directly inside,
with a conglomeration of odds and ends piled behind them.

"He surely wouldn't put them there," she objected, at
the same time idly poking an experimental finger here and
there amid the piled rubbish. "We'd better open his luggage."

As she withdrew her hand, a mesh of the net caught on
the wrist watch she always wore, and they tumbled out,
pulling some of the accumulated odds and ends with them.
Had a hooded cobra suddenly reared its head within the
cupboard Tam could not have looked more utterly petri-
fied—for the displaced articles had bared a piece of gleam-
ing silk, brocaded in pale pink water lilies.

For a second the room whirled dizzily and Fitzharris
caught at her shoulder; he thought she was going to faint.

"What the blue-hell—" He spluttered. "What's gone
wrong?"

She simply pointed to the silvery silk, forgetting that it could not hold the same significance for him as for her. While he still stared at her, entirely uncomprehending, Tam fought for and regained full self control. Reaching into the depths of the cupboard she grasped the betraying patch of silk.

It was firmly wedged into place and resisted her effort for a second. Then it came out onto the littered floor—unrolling, so that the objects around which it had been wrapped lay, nakedly accusing, before their horrified eyes.

A woman's dainty silver slippers, stockings to match, sheer peach-colored undergarments—not even the embroidered garters described by Leslie Carew's maid were missing.

The horrid meaning of the find was evident, now, even to Fitzharris, who had recalled reading of the much-searched-for articles.

"Oakley!" he gasped. "God—it's not possible!"

"Then what are they doing here?" Tam desperately demanded. "Yet you're right—I can't believe it, I won't!"

She sprang to her feet, glaring at the equally horrified Fitzharris as if the fault were his.

"Think back to the night of the murder—tell me everything that happened."

"Why—why—" He stammered, whereat the usually self-contained Tam stamped an enraged foot on the sadly littered floor.

"Don't stare like a goggle-eyed fish—tell me exactly what you both did, between dinner time and the hour you and he found Leslie's body in the summer house."

With an effort of will Fitzharris forced his tongue into coherent speech.

"I'm not a member of the country club, but I had two tickets for the dance and invited Oakley to go along. After dinner we smoked and puttered about the house till, say

9:30 or a bit later, then drifted up to the club. Some men we both knew were on the veranda; we all talked for a little, then adjourned to the smoking room for liquid refreshments. It was thundering hot, if you remember, and we decided against dancing. Then the wife of one of our friends sent word her party was short two men—asked him to join her and bring along some other man who danced. He collared me, and we left the others still enjoying their drinks."

"What time was this?" Tam cut in.

"Somewhere between ten and the half hour—nearer the latter, I'd say."

"Yes. And then?"

"Well, I danced perhaps half a dozen numbers. Then a cute little partner took me out to her car for an extra special drink and we got to—er—talking; must have stayed out there quite some time. It was past twelve, say ten or twenty after, when little cutie's husband horned in and broke up our party. I went back to the smoking room, looking for Oakley, but he wasn't there.

"Then, only a few minutes later, he turned up, saying the club house was so infernally hot we'd better take a stroll and cool off. We did, walking slowly about, till the lights in the summer house made us think it on fire. We investigated—you know the rest."

"So, in plain English, you've no earthly idea where Oakley Calhoun was between, say ten-twenty and twenty minutes past twelve—two hours—and the very two hours during which Leslie was murdered and her body tricked out in all that flaunting mockery of death."

They stared at each other, each silently weighing the incredible possibility. It was Tam who spoke first.

"No, I will not believe it! He was my friend." But there was more stubborn loyalty than conviction in her voice.

"Even to think it makes me feel a cad," Fitzharris muttered. "But I can't forget he'd a sort of motive."

"A motive?" Tam echoed blankly.

"A sort of a one," he helplessly repeated. "The kind one reads about—a long-standing grievance—avenging a wrong one person's done to another person that you loved."

"You mean his old friend Eric Carew?"

"Yes. It's common talk that Leslie drove him to suicide."

"You think he may have brooded over that, and when a sudden opportunity offered, paid off Eric's score?"

"I can't help remembering how bitterly he's spoken of his dead friend's widow."

"Not good enough! He'd need a stronger motive to kill—besides—"

Her expression suddenly lightened under the relief of a new thought. "From what you know of Calhoun, don't you believe he'd be satisfied with the mere fact of an enemy's death? Can you see him turning the body into a side show?"

"No! That hint's of a smaller nature— Calhoun may have been ruthless, but he was never petty!"

"So I believed. Mr. Fitzharris, you and I have got to take his innocence for granted—and prove it in the one certain way, by finding the actual murderer!"

For once in her life, Tam planned on deliberately concealing evidence from the police. The incriminating contents of the cupboard must remain a secret between Calhoun's two friends until such time as they were in a position to prove it was not to his guilt they pointed. Still—how account for the presence of those incriminating garments? Why, since he had them, had he not told her?

It was a very much depressed Tam who, next morning, rang Inspector McCoy at headquarters and asked for news. His answering voice was almost aggressively cheerful.

"Caught your Queen of Hearts late last night," he glee-fully chortled. "Finally traced her through bribing the sweetheart of a near-by expressman into worming out of him where he'd taken the disappearing lady of the apartment house and her trunks. Seems she and Miles split when they feared we were closing in on them, so he's escaped us up to now. But she's here. Been on the grill ever since we caught her, and is about ready to talk. Streak down here if you want to be in at the finish."

She obeyed as literally as the speed restrictions permitted, and reached McCoy's office in plenty of time to hear the Queen of Hearts' mingled confession and denial.

The woman was not of a fiber strong enough to withstand a night of merciless questioning at the hands of the police, and her drug-shattered nerves had shrieked for the relief held out as a reward for frank confession. By the time Tam arrived, the promised dose of morphine had begun to take effect and the woman's ravaged face, now tear-stained and haggard from the long ordeal, showed signs of returning strength and courage.

"Now, Mrs. Chadwick—you admit your real name is Lydia Chadwick, formerly Lydia Lord?" McCoy commenced, then, after her nod of assent, went on. "You understand that what you say is to be taken down in the form of a statement which you'll be required to sign before witnesses?" Again she only nodded, and he opened direct fire.

"You were your sister's mysterious supper guest, on the night she was shot?"

"Yes."

"Now, start at the beginning, please, and tell us what led up to that secret meeting between you two."

For an instant Lydia Chadwick hesitated, apparently more because of uncertainty where to begin than because of any intense reluctance.

"You know that my father and husband had quarreled years ago, and that Leslie and I were forbidden to meet or even write."

"Sure, we know that; go ahead."

"There wasn't any use of openly opposing my father, but we never obeyed him. Leslie and I always kept in touch through Rosamond Forbes, who was my best friend. Sometimes we didn't see one another for long periods of time, because my husband's operations took him to different cities and I nearly always went along; but as I tell you, we always wrote.

"Then, about four years ago, Miles and I got into difficulties with the Federal Narcotic agents, and after that things went from bad to worse—they're hell to shake off, those Federal men, once they've got you on their black list. We had to hide and dodge about so that I lost touch with both Rosamond and my sister. Of course I could have reached them at any time, even if they didn't know where I was, but I was afraid to write; a letter might so easily give a clue leading back to its sender.

"I suppose you know that, between us, we'd lost what money I had when we were married. I knew it was hopeless appealing to my father; so last spring, when things got downright desperate, I took the risk and wrote to Leslie under cover to Rosamond, asking for help. It seems she sent a cheque to the address I gave, but in the meantime we had reason to think the Federal agents were after us again, so we had to vamoose and I never received her cheque. Later on I wrote again, the letter miscarried and by the time it reached her we'd again moved on.

"Well, Miles and I were down inside our last dollar, when I finally phoned Leslie begging an appointment and help. We didn't dare meet at Dune House, both because of father's attitude, and because for all I knew the narcotic people might be watching it—they'd recently shown a renewed interest in us, and I couldn't tell how deep it might be. Leslie told me to come to the country club at ten o'clock. She'd engage a certain room which we both knew, one that had a French window opening on a terrace. She promised to have two thousand dollars in cash ready for me.

"Everything worked with perfect smoothness. Miles borrowed a car and drove me out, then waited up a side lane while I cut across the club grounds and gained the window of Room 14. There were so many people about that I don't think any one saw me, not to notice at least, and we had the first really sisterly talk in years."

"Why did Mrs. Carew insist on such pronounced secrecy?" McCoy asked as she paused to ask for, and receive, a cigarette.

"She knew I was wanted by the Federal agents and wasn't sure how close they might be on my trail. Poor kid, when she saw that I was hungry—I simply devoured all the supper she'd ordered—she actually cried. She vowed something had to be done to save me from such horrid straits. It was then she told me about having made a new will after she got my last letter, in which she left me thirty thousand.

"She also advised me to have Miles get in touch with the Joker, the man who ran the Fifty-Three Limited. We'd both known him in the past, and Leslie thought he could use Miles' services—she said we were welcome to mention her name. Then we talked over old times for a while, about the night club and the good times we'd both had there.

"Presently I asked about the man I'd read she was engaged to; and she flew off at a wild tangent, telling me how her mother-in-law had just that evening repeated some scandal she'd heard about Truxton Manning and a dancer named Inga Farrar. The elder Mrs. Carew had only heard of their association in California, but as it happened, Leslie herself had met the dancer in the Fifty-Three Limited, of course without suspecting that she'd ever been Manning's mistress. Now she jumped to the conclusion that the old affair was still going on under cover. She was perfectly furious."

"It wasn't that you quarreled about?" McCoy interjected.

"We didn't quarrel," Lydia retorted, with a resentful side glance. "We parted the best possible friends—having arranged to meet a few nights later at the Joker's club. I left as I'd come, through the French window, and joined Miles in the lane, where I told you he was waiting."

"And then you talked matters over," the inspector insinuated. "You told him about the new will—and both of you decided that thirty thousand would come in mighty handy. No good denying it—we know you went back, found your sister in the summer house and killed her!"

"That's a lie! You don't know anything of the kind!" Lydia told him with the utmost calmness. "If you possessed even a glimmer of human intelligence, you'd realize I couldn't ever come forward to claim my legacy, because if I did I'd be walking into the clutch of the narcotic agents."

16
What Lydia Knew

Before Inspector McCoy could adequately retaliate, pandemonium suddenly broke loose in the hall outside his door. A woman's high-pitched voice shrieked that she would go in, she'd like to see the brute that could stop her—while several masculine voices vainly attempted to soothe and pacify the enraged visitor.

Then someone thumped violently on the door panel, there was the sound of a short, sharp scuffle, and the door burst open to admit Rosamond Forbes—very much the worse for her encounter with the restraining hands of the police, but still triumphant.

"Sufferin' Saint Peter! What's the meaning of this?" McCoy demanded.

"Sorry, sir; we couldn't stop her." One of his men sheepishly apologized, wiping a trickle of blood from his lacerated cheek. "She fought like an inspired wildcat, and it's claws she has, not fingernails!"

Meanwhile Rosamond had darted across to her quietly watching friend, Lydia, about whom she flung a protecting arm, then turned defiantly to face the representatives of the law.

"This morning's paper told how you'd arrested Lydia for the murder of her sister. So I rushed in to tell you it wasn't true—she's no more guilty than I am!"

McCoy eyed her balefully. "Couldn't you have sent in your name and waited decent admission?" he barked at her.

"While you put Lydia through some hellish third degree? No, I couldn't!" Rosamond retorted, quite unabashed. "I told the man at the desk who I was and why I'd come, but he said you were questioning the prisoner and couldn't be disturbed until you'd finished. Naturally I didn't intend peacefully waiting while you wrung some false admission out of the poor girl, so I came in anyway, even if some idiots did try to stop me."

"So we noticed!" McCoy dryly observed. "Perhaps, now you're here, you won't mind telling us what brought you."

"I gave Lydia my sacred word of honor not to tell of certain things that occurred on the night Leslie was shot— she was afraid that if the police knew she'd been at the club, they'd begin suspecting her of the murder; and even if that didn't happen, news of her presence in Meadow Dale would put the Federal agents hot on her trail. Up to now, I've kept the promise not to tell, but it's time to break it, because I can prove she wasn't near the club at the hour the doctors say Leslie was killed!"

"How can you prove it?"

"By telling you where to look for certain witnesses, who'll swear to seeing Lydia miles away from Meadow Dale at that identical hour!"

"Let's hear about these witnesses who've kept such cautiously shut mouths up to now."

"Only because they've no idea who she is," Rosamond snapped at him. "If you'll only keep quiet for five minutes, I'll tell you exactly what happened. I told you I left the club house at about 9:30. Well, that was perfectly true, I only lied in saying I'd gone directly home. Actually, I was so mad I let my car whoop down the highway for I can't say how many miles; then, when I'd calmed down a little,

I turned back and presently, say about twenty minutes to eleven, I saw a stalled car headed away from Meadow Dale. A man and woman were fussing around it, and when my headlights struck them I recognized Lydia and her husband.

"Well, to get to those witnesses I spoke of—I turned back and towed their car, until we came to a garage that was still open for repair work. By that time it was a little after eleven and we were miles away from Meadow Dale. There were two men in the garage and several others hanging around it—I can drive you to the place, though I can't tell you its precise location offhand—and once those men see us, they'll confirm what I say. Naturally they haven't come forward, because they'd no reason to connect that particular car with a murder that happened in the next county."

"Sounds plausible," McCoy admitted after a little thought. "And it can easily be checked up. I suppose the Chadwicks got their car fixed so they could go on, and it was when you'd almost reached Meadow Dale on the way back that you had trouble with that flat."

"Exactly," Rosamond confirmed. "And now that you know the truth, I suppose you'll stop persecuting poor Lydia."

It was Lydia herself who gave the answer before McCoy could properly frame it:

"Sorry, darling, but you've missed one little detail—it's not one murder they're holding me for, but two."

"Two?" her friend echoed on a note of consternation.

"Yes!" Lydia nodded. "And the worst of it is, *I'm guilty of the second one!*"

For an instant no one spoke. Then Rosamond burst into a storm of disbelief which Lydia quietly silenced.

"I told them I'd talk if they gave me some morphine—they kept their half of the bargain, and I intend keeping

mine! Mostly because I'm so deadly tired of dodging the
law that life's not worth the constant effort—not the way
I've lived it these last few years, anyway."

She turned to directly face Inspector McCoy.

"Ask any questions you like—only, before you begin,
I'd like to say that I'd no intention of killing Oakley Calhoun. I scarcely knew him; that part was a regrettable
accident."

"But you did mean to kill Tam O'Brien?"

"Oh, yes! I thought she was on our trail about drug
selling. Maybe the morphine has blurred my brain a little,
or perhaps the constant dodging has given me a fear-com-
plex—anyway, I was terrified of her. And it never occurred
to me that her interest in the Queen of Hearts only had to
do with Leslie's murder—I had no earthly reason to suppose she could connect me with that."

She seemed utterly ashamed of the act she had confessed. She never once glanced toward the listening Tam
o' Shanter.

"You see, Miles had heard about her; she's pretty well
known in the underworld, and she'd been pointed out to
him. So he recognized her the day he visited Dune House,
and her being there prevented his carrying out the scheme
that had already taken him to see my father. He had intended telling about Leslie's new will, insisting on their
looking for it, and then offering to settle for half the
amount named, quietly handed over without due process
of law. We thought, in that way, we'd avoid running against
the Federal agents. But the plan savored of blackmail and
Miles didn't dare broach it before a detective.

"Later, Rosamond came to the club to tell me Tam o'
Shanter was searching for me; and that she, Rosamond,
had given her the picture of one of our girlhood chums,
with my name written on it. She thought it a great joke,
and insisted on taking me over to meet the detective who

was hunting the original of that photograph while never dreaming I was the woman she really wanted.

"Nothing much happened then. But they came again the following night, and determinedly attached themselves to me—I realized, by the way Mr. Calhoun insisted on retaining possession of the white booth and managed to keep the cocaine matches out of my reach, that he suspected something. And when I saw my husband, Miles, come in and start across to join us, not recognizing the two I was with because they had their backs turned, I pretended to see a vision or something and acted so I warned him off.

"By that time I was sure they were after us. Tam o' Shanter had to be stopped, no matter how. The Joker had agreed to take Miles into a sort of outside partnership in the drug distributing part of his business, and I couldn't let her spoil the only real chance Miles had had in years. So I went home as soon as I could, found Miles already there, and persuaded him to try to eliminate her interference once for all. He drew the line at open murder, swearing if they knew their pet had been purposely killed, the whole police force would vow undying vengeance and our lives wouldn't be worth ten cents—they'd never rest till they'd run down her slayers. We arranged things to look like an accident—but the scheme miscarried. And next night Tam o' Shanter and Calhoun calmly showed up at the club.

"I was desperate. She *had* to be put out of the way. So I—used a poison I'd brought with me in case I could find a chance to administer it. You probably pretty well know what happened. I got her away by phoning Miles to call the club and pretend he was on long distance wanting to speak to Miss O'Brien; then, after I'd dropped the poison in her cup while Calhoun was at the cigar counter, they changed places and he drank the wrong coffee."

She stopped a second, then added with a certain hopeless finality: "That's all! I've told you everything. And

Miles had nothing to do with it. As I told you, he balked at actual murder, and he didn't even know why I asked him to telephone Tam o' Shanter."

"I think the law will consider him an accessory both before and after the crime," McCoy told her sternly. "You'll have to tell us where to find him."

"Oh, no! I agreed to confess my own sins—nothing was said about including Miles. Besides, I don't know where he is, I couldn't tell you if I wanted to. Now, if you'll let me sign that statement and go some place where I can rest—I'm so hideously tired."

She seemed to have already lost all interest in life and barely listened to the reading over of her long confession. When she had signed it, and a prison matron had led her away, Rosamond Forbes was requested to accompany two police officials to the garage where she claimed the Chadwick car had undergone repairs on the night of the murder. She was too subdued by the discovery of her friend's guilt to offer an objection and departed with the utmost meekness.

"Well, here I am with my case pretty well cleared up, while you're as much in the dark as ever," McCoy complacently remarked as he settled to the enjoyment of one of his beloved cigars.

"Not quite that," Tam smiled at him. "At least, I know Lydia and Rosamond had nothing to do with Leslie's death."

"A lot *that* helps!" He lapsed into contented meditation, presently emerging with a satisfied chuckle. "Pleasant change, to find you dead in the wrong for once, Miss Lady-sleuth—Calhoun's murder had nothing whatever to do with the earlier one on Long Island."

"Did I ever claim to be infallible?" she responded, not in the least ruffled by his triumph. "Besides I was only mistaken in the motive, not in the connection. If I hadn't been on Lydia's trail because of her sister's violent death, she'd never have got the idea I was interested in her precious husband's drug activities. Singular type, isn't she? One would think her too mortally tired of life and her own drug slavery, ever to be capable of planning and executing a murder."

"That's the worst of drug addicts; you never can tell what they will or won't do. Apt to be strong or weak in the most unexpected places!" McCoy feelingly complained. "Personally, while I'm no doctor, I doubt if she'll ever live to face a trial. Strikes me as physically pretty far gone; she's evidently been using morphine for years. By the bye, did you get what she let slip about the Joker's being active in the drug trade? That's information worth passing on to the narcotic agents."

Tam nodded. "Yes, I've known about it all along."

"Oh, you have, have you? And never let out a peep?"

"My hands were tied by the pledge Lieutenant Fisk gave and I seconded."

"Most likely you'll be running into him at the Fifty-Three Limited, now he's got the tip elsewhere."

"What makes you think I'm still interested there?"

"Haven't found the Ace of Diamonds, have you?" he retorted. "And I can't see you dropping the trail until you do."

Lydia's confession had so confused the issues on the original murder case that Tam felt decidedly fogged. But of one thing she still remained sure, and that was her own wish to keep Inga Farrar out of the investigation. As deliberate falsehood formed no part of her program, she parted from McCoy as speedily as possible and drove slowly homeward, a prey to the most unwonted depression.

In the light of her newer knowledge, Oakley Calhoun's death seemed such a doubly unnecessary waste. Then thoughts of him automatically recalled the contents of the

cupboard in his room at the Meadow Dale, and added to
her sense of hopeless failure. For a moment or two she
even entertained a fear of his possible guilt; then loyalty
to his memory sent it scurrying and she determinedly settled to a revisal of the evidence collected, and a desperate
search for some as yet unconsidered suspect.

Just at that point a block in the traffic held her inactive
for several minutes and during the wait her eyes rested
idly on the rear of a car ahead. She was unaware of really
seeing it, but slowly her subjective self forced upward into
her conscious mind a sense of something familiar, something seen before. "990083"—

She found herself staring at the rear license plate, displayed on the car ahead. Its two first and last numbers
were the same as those on the white wrapping paper found
tucked under Leslie Carew's dead feet.

As the green light flashed on, Tam was too dazed to
obey its signal. Her car remained stationary until the hearty
abuse of other drivers whose way she was blocking recalled
her to a sense of her immediate surroundings and she remembered to take advantage of the green traffic light.

Her predominant feeling was one of amazement that
she had not sooner guessed the meaning of those perplexing numbers. Wasn't the white oblong of the general size
and shape of an automobile license plate? How utterly stupid never to have noticed the resemblance—though perhaps the fact that both date and classifying letter had been
omitted partly accounted for her never having thought of
what now seemed an almost obvious conclusion.

Because of that same omission of a date, Tam felt it
wiser to begin with the current year and work backward.
The present owner of the car licensed under the number
"997033" turned out to be a Greek candy merchant of
Brooklyn, whom the wildest flight of fancy failed to connect with the Meadow Dale Country Club or Leslie Carew.

The owners of the cryptic murder number for one, two, and three years back, proved equally unpromising, though she realized they would all have to be carefully investigated if search through the license files failed to unearth a contact. But in the record of four years back came a distinct surprise—in 1926, Leslie Carew's own private car had borne the license number "997033."

Whatever name Tam had vaguely expected to encounter, it had certainly not been that of the murder-victim herself. And for a little she felt more completely at sea than ever.

From the very commencement of the case, she had firmly believed that none of the articles arranged on or near Leslie's body were meaningless—that each had a significance of its own, could she but read it. And if so with the other things, so also with the number borne by Leslie's car in 1926. Some secret, perhaps only known to murderer and victim, lay hidden in those six printed figures. But how to go about the discovering of that secret was a horse of quite another color. Tam seemed minus the shadow of a guiding clue.

Yet was she? Did not the thread through the labyrinth lie somewhere amid the other articles of the bizarre death scene?

One by one she ran them over in her mind—was there not some suggested clue, some hair-fine connection? Lights, flower, gauze? Hardly indicative, any of them. The sprinkled sugar which possibly stood for morphine? That was a little better; it might conceivably point toward the Fifty-Three Limited. Strange how every trail seemed sooner or later to lead to that same club! Tam's Celtic blood quickened with something resembling a premonitory thrill—would not the key to the mystery's final solution be found within its doors?

Contrary to her usual custom of making few if any notes or sketches from which to work, she next drew five rough sketches of the cards found in Leslie's passive fingers and slowly studied the result

The Ace of Diamonds? According to her present belief Inga, the owner of that particular card, had told the truth when she declared that, though she had taken her pistol to the country club with the full intention of using it if Leslie refused to resign the man whom she, Inga, herself loved, her nerve had been unequal to the actual deed and she had fled, leaving the weapon for someone else to find and use.

The Queen of Hearts? Tam saw no reason for believing that Lydia would have denied one murder while admitting the other, unless she was telling the truth—also, if the garage men who, by Rosamond's story, had repaired the Chadwick car practically at the hour of Leslie's death, identified Lydia, she would be supplied with an unanswerable alibi.

The Joker? Personally Tam knew almost nothing about him, but at present she could think of no sensible reason why he should desire Leslie's death.

Thus, with three cards more or less disposed of, there remained only the Jack of Spades and the Tray of Diamonds. Did they also designate members of the Fifty-Three Limited? And was the answer to the riddle of "997038" known to one or both of them? It seemed that once again the trail led back to the Fifty-Three Limited.

17

The Jack of Spades

When Tam arrived at the night club, the hour was still too early for it to be in active operation. But waiters and other employees were already preparing for the approaching busy hours.

Almost the first person she saw was the Joker, deep in troubled consultation with Lieutenant Fisk, whose continued presence the club proprietor seriously resented. His difficulties failed to interest Tam in the least and she unhesitatingly interrupted them with a request.

"Mr. Davis, I'd like a private interview with any of your employees who have been with you for four years or longer. Lieutenant Fisk will vouch for the fact that I'm working in the interests of the police."

It seemed that the number of people who had been with the Joker for so long a time was strictly limited. He was able to discover only three, and from the first two, a chef's assistant and a cleaning woman, Tam gained no useful information whatever.

The third employee who entered the small private room where the Joker had invited her to carry on her desired interviews, was an elderly, attenuated waiter, whose look of disillusioned intelligence made her hope for better results. She motioned him to a chair, then asked: "Exactly how long have you worked here?"

"Almost six years," he told her wearily.

"That's an unusual length of time for any night club to remain in existence."

"Yes. But the Fifty-Three Limited hasn't ever been like the rest. It started in 1919, directly after prohibition went into force, as a private club. And when the Joker took it over—he was only manager at first, you know—he continued running it along exclusive lines and never let in the general public."

"Probably that's why it's lasted so long. Now, getting down to what I want to learn; Did you know Leslie Carew?"

"Of course, Miss, we all knew her, both by name and as the Tray of Diamonds. She used to stage parties that were the gayest ever held here."

"Did you also know her husband?"

"Slightly. He never came often, and he put a damper on the fun when he did come along."

"Can you remember back, clearly enough to give me a description of Mrs. Carew's most intimate friends, say, about four years ago?"

He did not answer immediately, evidently trying to recall people and events of the time she named.

"It's a little hard to be certain of things that happened so long ago," he finally acknowledged. "If I'm not mistaken, her sister, Mrs. Chadwick, stopped coming to the club about that time. But Mrs. Forbes and her husband were among our most regular patrons. Of course that was long before the divorce that's washed so much dirty linen. Then, let me see, there were several others, who mostly came with Mrs. Carew."

He gave a list of seven or eight names, none of which in the least enlightened his questioner, then came an embarrassed pause; there was something he hesitated about revealing.

"Better not hold back any facts," Tam finally advised. "When a murder is being investigated, the police don't appreciate too much discretion."

"It can't do any harm to tell now, so long afterwards, when she's dead and all of that," the veteran waiter decided. "You see, at one time Mrs. Carew didn't want the affair talked about, and she paid us all pretty heavily not to mention it."

"What affair?" Tam demanded, conscious of a distinct hope that she was at long last on the right trail.

"About the Jack of Spades, Miss. That's the only name we ever knew him by."

"Tell me everything you can possibly remember," she prompted him with keenest interest. Was not the card he mentioned one of those found in Leslie's dead hand?

"I'll have to explain a little about Mrs. Carew first," he apologized. "You see, she wasn't like most of our ladies, who generally come right along with the same escort. Not that they don't change them more or less often," he added with due regard for strict accuracy. "But there's mostly only one or two regular ones at the same time. Mrs. Carew was different; she never came twice running with the same man, and almost never alone with anybody. She liked big parties, the bigger the better, and from watching I got the idea that what she most liked was to have a lot of men admiring and flattering her, all together—she didn't seem to much care for what you might call private love-making. This, you understand, was during the time I first came here to work. Then, I think it was in 1926, she changed entirely and started being always with the man known as the Jack of Spades.

"Often and often they came alone, just by themselves. But if there was a party he was always included, except when Mr. Carew was with them—I noticed the two men

were never with her at the same time. That's what made us
think the affair must be downright serious."

"Can you describe this Jack of Spades?"

"Easily, Miss; he wasn't the sort you'd be likely to forget. First of all, he was very young, in his early twenties
I'd say at a guess; and tall, he must have been well over
six feet and big-framed to match. Astonishing handsome,
Miss, blond and blue-eyed and always laughing as if he
hadn't a care in the world—that is, until toward the last;
he changed a lot before he dropped out."

"Precisely when did that happen?"

"Not until after Mr. Carew killed himself. Just let me
think a minute, Miss. The time when the Jack of Spades
first started coming here was about four years ago, I'd say,
and he kept on being with Mrs. Carew for a good year and
a half. That brings us to a few months after her husband's
death—it must have been about two and a half years ago
that he all of a sudden dropped out."

"You said just now that he changed a good deal before
that happened."

"Yes, Miss, a lot." He glanced at her dubiously, then
decided on frankness. "I think it was the morphine got
him, Miss. We get used to reading the signs here, and I'm
pretty sure he'd become an addict."

"Did none of you ever get a clue to the Jack of Spade's
real name?"

"Never, Miss, though we were all curious. I remember
watching the Sunday papers to see if his picture wouldn't
be shown amongst the society bigwigs—lots of our other
patrons were often pictured in the social news. But never
the Jack of Spades."

"Would you say he was wealthy, of the same general
class as Mrs. Carew?"

"I don't quite know, Miss. He always handled money
very free, but his clothes hadn't precisely the right look—

not that they weren't expensive, it was more as if he didn't rightly know how to wear them—like you sometimes notice with a boy that's grown up in the country, Miss."

That was about the sum of what she could learn concerning the Jack of Spades. And as to what real name lurked behind the fanciful designation she could hazard not even a guess. His description fitted no one of whom she had hitherto heard during the course of the investigation, and it seemed more than probable that he had passed completely out of Leslie's life and was not even remotely connected with her untimely end. Still—if so, why was his namecard among those placed in her hand, presumably by her murderer?

She determined to at least pursue his trail to the vanishing point, and chose Dr. Ramsey as her most promising informant. Taking the precaution to first telephone for an appointment, she drove out to Meadow Dale and exhaustively questioned him about Leslie's older friends. But he quite failed to remember anyone at all answering the old waiter's description of the Jack of Spades.

"Leslie always liked tall men, I noticed that myself," he remarked in conclusion. "But I never thought she favored one man friend beyond the others. It was admiration in bulk that most appealed to her, the greater the bulk the better. But I can't say I remember any yellow-haired young giant dancing especial attendance."

They let the subject drop at that, and discussed Lydia Chadwick's arrest and confession.

"I understand she was taken through a police stool-pigeon," Tam explained. "But up to the time I left headquarters, nothing had been heard of her husband.

"I certainly hope they catch him!" The doctor spoke with an almost vicious belligerence. "He's far more to blame than poor Lydia—teaching her to use morphine was probably his work, and without that she'd never have killed anybody. It's horrible how drugs destroy a victim's real nature! Well, at least she was innocent of her sister's murder; I was right about that. Oh, by the way, you're not giving any attention to Manning's suspicions against Sarah Carew, are you?"

"Not at the moment. Why?"

"Only because if you're wasting time over her, I wanted to warn you I'd learned where she spent those unaccounted-for hours on the night of the dance. I put some questions, without her suspecting what I was after, and she told me how Leslie's behavior on that night drove her into seeking a sort of spiritual consolation from her dead son—she spent a large part of the night at Eric's grave."

On Tam's mental list of possible sources of information, the maid Anice came second. So when her interview with the coroner was over, she proceeded to Dune House and, ignoring the main entrance, drove around to a rear door, where she inquired for Anice.

To avoid being overheard, Tam left her car and led the pleasantly flustered maid down a little side path, where they were safe from interruption.

When she had finished repeating the waiter's word picture of the Jack of Spades, Anice surprised her by an amused laugh.

"Why, it's not one of Mrs. Carew's friends you're describing, Miss—it's only Jack, the chauffeur!"

At the words Tam almost gasped—the name Jack—chauffeur—license number—surely the evidence was at last beginning to link.

"You're sure of that?"

"Oh, yes, Miss! Jack was ever so tall, 'way over six feet, and handsome! He'd the bluest eyes and the yellowest hair ever you saw!"

"And this Jack drove Mrs. Carew's own car about four years ago?"

Anice quite openly counted back on her fingers. "Yes, Miss. It doesn't seem so long ago, but now I come to think, he came to us before Mr. Eric died."

"And afterwards?"

"Oh, he was here for quite a while. Until he started drinking or something and Mrs. Leslie had to discharge him. Oh, there's Mrs. Carew calling me; I'll have to run."

Evidently their privacy was less secure than Tam had supposed, and before she could put another question Anice had fled in the direction of the calling voice. Her next point of inquiry was the country club, for knowing that Dorcas Shell had been the Carew housekeeper during the time this mysterious Jack of Spades had acted as Leslie's private chauffeur, she expected to obtain fuller details from her.

Arrived at the club, she found the stewardess was off duty. But Scanlan, as usual, was more than ready to talk.

"Do you know where I can find Dorcas?" she asked. Scanlan himself didn't, but he sent for the pleasant-faced stewardess with whom Tam had talked once at the beginning of the inquiry, and she was able to tell them that Dorcas had gone to see about the closing of her cottage, whose tenant meant vacating it on the first of next month.

"I didn't realize she was a land owner." Tam idly fished for information. "Which is her cottage?"

"The one Mr. Fitzharris and the nice gentleman who got killed, lived in, Miss."

"Why I know that cottage; it is a charming little place. I wonder Dorcas doesn't live in it herself."

"Most likely she can't afford to, except in the winter when nobody'd rent it. You see when her son was sick so long, Dorcas used up all her savings on doctors and such— it was only afterwards that an uncle left her this cottage, or I expect it would have gone, too."

Tam next inquired if either of them knew how she could reach Owen Fitzharris and was told that at the moment he was away, having gone on an overnight fishing trip with some other club members.

Disappointed by the news, Tam decided on following Dorcas down to the cottage, even if Fitzharris himself was beyond reach. It was almost dusk as she parked the car outside the cottage gate and walked thoughtfully up the flower-bordered path.

Would the Jack of Spades prove as futile a clue as all the others, or could Dorcas tell her enough facts concerning him to bring the man out of the four-year-old mist obscuring his personality and make him live either in the present or the very recent past?

The front door stood wide open and Tam entered. There was no one in sight, and though the dusk was encroaching like a soft, impalpable presence, no lights burned. Perfect quiet lay over the little house; there was no sound of movement as Tam stood listening—yet something drew her eyes to the steep stairway leading up to the second floor. The next instant she realized that a tiny swirl of smoke had eddied past her face, bringing the odor of burning cloth.

She never quite knew what kept her silent, sent her stealthily up the steep staircase where the odor of burning cloth strengthened with each ascending step. Oakley Calhoun's door was almost closed, but through the crack came a wisp of the malodorous smoke and crossing to it on tip-toe she peered cautiously, inside.

On the hearth directly opposite, a small fire was burning; and before it, like some eerie priestess of Agni, the Fire-God, knelt Dorcas Snell—a pair of great shears that caught and redly answered the fire's glow in one hand, in the other a length of silvery brocaded cloth, which she was quietly shredding into pieces small enough to feed the flames without danger of smothering them.

As the full significance of the scene penetrated to her startled consciousness, Tam darted silently across the dusky room, caught the remaining silk from Dorcas' un-resisting hand and with a hastily snatched rug, struggled to beat out the fire before it could consume the articles already smoldering in its hearth.

"I've suspected all along!" Tam cried. "You don't cheat me of the evidence I need now!"

For the moment she ignored the woman herself, only the saving of the irreplaceable evidence engrossed her—a carelessness for which she came near paying very dearly. For as the flames died under the smothering rug, a sharply caught breath made her turn, barely in time to evade a savage downward thrust of the lifted shears, held dagger-wise.

There was a brief, totally silent struggle, that left Dorcas again crouched on the hearth, this time nursing an arm strained as Tam forcibly deprived her of the shears.

For a moment Tam stood, her brain whirling dizzily, as she strove to realize and coordinate all the meanings of the scene. Then she slowly crossed to the old-fashioned lamp on the centre table and lighted it, one eye remaining watchfully on the small, bent figure on the hearth.

"So the Jack of Spades was your son—the son who died two years ago." It was a bow drawn very much at a venture, but the result proved its accuracy of aim.

"Died because of what she'd done to him—died like a mongrel cur tossed in the gutter!" Her low voice was almost a snarl, ominous, menacing, yet threaded with grief.

"And so you killed her." Tam spoke on a matter of fact note, as though the deed were nothing uncommon; a simple evening of the score.

"Yes." Dorcas' grey head nodded affirmation. "I'd often longed to punish her, but I'd never known how to do it—until that dancing woman showed me the way. She threw away her pistol and ran as if she couldn't face Leslie's taunts—it seemed such a pity to let it lie there not used at all—when they'd both gone, I just picked it up

Dorcas knelt before the open fire, feeding to the flames something which Tam could not at first identify

and followed her to the summer house. She never thought
of fearing me or looking at what I held. It was easy! Oh,
very easy!"

"But after all, do you think you're quite fair in blaming
her for Jack's death? He was a grown man, wasn't he?"

"What's that you're saying?" Dorcas lifted burning eyes
to hers. "He was no more than a boy, I tell you! A beautiful, innocent boy—she took him and broke him, as you
and I wouldn't do to a dog."

"If you were right there in the house, why didn't you
stop it in the beginning—before he'd really lost his head?"

Tam, every nerve keyed wire-taught, was hinting,
searching, feeling for a way to open the gates of the mother's surcharged heart.

"Oh, the beginning—" Dorcas appeared to be going
back through the years to a time when her boy had been
wholly her own.

Just then Tam caught a distracting sound from out-
of-doors; someone was merrily whistling as he tramped
crunchingly up the gravel path. Thanking her stars for the
other's momentary excursion into the past, Tam stole to
the window. There was light enough left to show her that
the shrill whistler was Owen Fitzharris; something must
have gone wrong with his fishing trip.

For a second, Tam almost despaired. If he came noisily
barging into the house it would almost certainly break the
thrall-like spell under which Dorcas seemed to have fall-
en—they might never get her full confession at all. Yet if
only she could secure Fitzharris as a witness! Spurred by
the thought, she leaned perilously from the open window,
waving a frantic hand until she had caught his attention,
then signing him to silence.

He stood staring up at her, looking positively stupid
from sheer noncomprehension until her pantomime began
to enlighten him; slowly it dawned that she was trying

to mutely tell him there was something going on in that upper room which it behooved him to witness—mutely warning him that stealth was supremely necessary.

When he had finally nodded his understanding and started elaborately tiptoeing toward the front door, she drew back from the window and turned, fearful that the interlude had destroyed her chance of extracting the truth from Dorcas. But the old stewardess did not seem aware of anything outside her own thoughts—those and a vague communion with Tam's voice; for she now seemed hardly conscious of the other's actual presence.

18
Dorcas' Story

"The beginning—" she was softly repeating to herself. "I wonder when that was? Perhaps a long time before I suspected anything; mothers are very blind about their sons, I think, and he was such a careless, happy-go-lucky youngling—I never realized he was old enough to catch a woman's fancy—stupid, wasn't I? But then, to me he was only a baby, not arrived at manhood at all.

"I knew Leslie'd never let anyone else drive her, especially when she was alone in the car. But I just thought it was because he was so strong and sure at the wheel; I never dreamt of any personal reason."

"You must have been astonished when you learned they went places together," Tam prompted, ever so gently.

"Yes. It seemed so odd—for as I told you, I hadn't realized him as a man. Then, going through his room, I found a suit of evening clothes and I couldn't understand why he should want them. Jack hated lying, he always had, even as a small thing who'd confess his badness with his little lips quivering because of the whipping he knew he'd get. I suppose it was that, his hating so to lie, that made him tell me how Mrs. Carew bought the clothes for him so he could take her into a night club where she liked going. She felt safer with a big strong man she knew she could trust, he said.

"That was the first I heard about the Joker's card-club. I guess he told me about it to sort of keep me from asking other questions he didn't want to answer. I heard how he was named the Jack of Spades and Mrs. Leslie the Tray of Diamonds, and about the man they called the Joker—it all sounded innocent enough, told as he told it, with his gay laugh ringing in between the words— only, I couldn't make it seem right for him to mix with people so much above him. It seemed harm must come of it, and it did, oh, it did!"

"What sort of harm?" Tam's beautiful voice was only a guiding whisper, holding no urgency and no demand.

"First, Jack began to lose his wonderful health. Not that he was sick, exactly, just sometimes heavy and dull-eyed and again full of mischief and fun that seemed sort of feverish. Of course I'd no inkling of drugs then. I only thought it was the late hours and that perhaps he drank more than he should.

"It was Mr. Eric who woke me up. Some way, he'd found out about their—friendship—and he'd more sense than I had; he realized what it meant, realized the black treachery going on in his house. I've never told before, not even to Jack, but I know that's why he killed himself—he couldn't stand what his wife had done to him—his wife, and—my son!"

There was a silence which Tam dared not break. She only ventured a glance toward the half shut door and was rewarded by sight of Fitzharris' appalled face just outside. At least there was a witness to this eerie confession, this laying bare of a dead love. Presently Dorcas went on speaking—who could tell what relief this open telling of the by-gone grief, that had never really eased, afforded the pent misery of the years between?

"That woke me in earnest and I tried to stop them—as well plead with a raging fire not to burn! She had lighted a blaze that consumed all his softer self—and besides, I know now that morphine had already started its black work of destruction. He grew worse and worse; they took to quarreling, then she discharged him just as she would any other servant who'd displeased her. And he—poor boy— he couldn't accept being tossed aside like something she'd used and tired of. You see, he'd given her a boy's first love, it meant all in all to him, but to her—well, he was big and handsome; he amused her, until the morphine she'd taught him to use began destroying his looks. That was all she'd ever really cared for.

"She wouldn't see him—returned his letters unopened, and he took to using more of the drug, in bigger doses— it couldn't go on like that, something had to give! I was afraid it would be his reason, but it wasn't that—his body broke instead. He'd wrecked himself, though the blame wasn't really his; it lay at her door.

"He was sick for months. I knew he was dying, and by that time all my money was gone. I put my pride away and wrote her, begging for help. Do you think she gave it?" Dorcas vented a low tortured laugh that echoed from the eaves as though a multitude of hag-ridden spirits mocked at their own misery. "She answered that no one could expect her to support all the discharged servants who happened to fall ill after leaving her employ—there were plenty of charities in the city, let me apply to them!

"I didn't mean Jack to see that letter. But morphine addicts have a queer kind of cunning—he managed to find and read it, and I think it crazed him. That night he stole out, half dressed, while I snatched a little sleep—I never saw him again—not alive, that is. For two days and nights I searched, frozen, almost without food, then I found him—found him naked on a marble slab at the morgue in the city! Do you wonder that I hated her?

"After she was dead and lying there, so soft and pretty in her shiny dress, I remembered how Jack had lain in the morgue under the pitiless icy drip of the water—and I planned to strip her as he'd been stripped—I knew how proud she was, knew that being exposed like that to all the curious eyes I meant calling, would hurt her worse than death itself!

"There must be a soft streak in me, for I couldn't quite do it. After everything was ready, and I'd lighted the candles so all her friends from the club should come and see her as she really was, with cards and wine and morphine—that soft streak made me tear the gauze from her dress and wrap it around her. And the little hole over her heart, some way I didn't like to look at it—it seemed a small mouth that cried blood—so I covered it with the flower I'd brought out to put in her hair.

"Everybody wondered why she was fixed like that—it was mostly because just killing her didn't seem enough. I wanted to shame her as she'd shamed my boy."

"But why did you put those cards in her hand? And how did you know about those others, the Ace of Diamonds and Queen of Hearts?" Tam risked the question, sure that Dorcas was bound to realize her position soon, in any case.

"The Joker, and Jack's card, and hers, I already knew; he'd told me about them long ago. The other two I got just that night, through hearing the sisters talking. I listened more than I let anybody know. They reminded each other what good times they used to have, and Leslie urged Lydia to come back and told how she'd paid to have her old card, the Queen of Hearts, saved for her. Then, later on, Leslie told her about the dancer Mr. Manning used to love, and she mentioned her getting the Ace of Diamonds' card and vowed she shouldn't keep it—she meant having her put out of the club, so she said.

"When Inga Farrar tried to make Leslie give back her lover, I found out who she was through what they said. And I thought if I lumped all the cards I knew about, together, and put them into her fingers, it would snarl everyone up and nobody'd ever suspect me at all—they'd think she was killed because of something that had to do with the Joker and his club."

"But if you wanted to avoid being suspected why did you put the license plate number on that piece of cardboard?"

"It's hard to say—exactly. In a way I felt the car that number belonged to was the start of everything between them. Without the long hours alone together in it they might never have grown such—friends—and putting it there like being honest, sort of showing the deepest reason for what I'd done, even though all the time I thought nobody'd ever read it right."

"And weren't you afraid someone would find the clothes in your house? Why didn't you throw them in the Sound?"

"They might have washed ashore. I didn't dare trust the water. So I brought them here, knowing both the men were up at the dance. I didn't think anybody'd have reason to poke into that little cupboard, and besides I'd got some blood on my dress and it was safer to wash it off in my own kitchen, where there weren't so many eyes as at the club."

"So tonight you planned burning them. Why wait until now?"

"The cottage hasn't been empty. Mr. Fitzharris and his friend were always in and out, and they'd a maid servant here daytimes—it seemed better to wait. Now the friend's dead, and Mr. Fitzharris away for the night, so I thought this would be a good time, especially as it was my night off duty, so my coming here wouldn't cause comment."

There was a long pause. Tam was waiting to see if Dorcas would add more of her own volition, and the latter was still apparently wrapped in the trancelike calm that had held her since that brief instant of desperate struggle.

How much did the woman realize of what had happened since then?

A sound from Fitzharris brought the answer. He had shifted his weight from one foot to the other and a board creaked complainingly.

"There's someone in the hall." Dorcas still spoke on a level note of calmness. But some somnambulant quality was gone from her voice; it was that of a person aware of her surroundings.

"Come in, Mr. Fitzharris." Tam knew the trance-spell was broken. "You heard Dorcas explaining why she killed Leslie Carew?"

"Yes." His breath caught sharply as he looked down at the bent, grey-haired figure still crouched on the hearth. "And I'm damned if I blame her!"

Dorcas raised sombre eyes to his; they contained no fear and no touch of anger, only a dreary, hopeless grief.

"I've not regretted, not for one single instant, for I think Jack rests better in his grave—when he comes to me now, in the long night-dreams, he's his old laughing self. I believe he's *glad* she can't ever destroy any other boy—as she destroyed him!"

It was months afterward, and Dips, his snub nose pressed flat against the window pane, was eyeing the bleak, wind-swept street with open disgust. Tam, curled on a rug before the cozily burning fire, indulged in day dreams.

"Ugh, there's a car stoppin'!" Dips presently announced. "Ain't sure e'ffen it's a weddin' or a funeral—it's that crammed with flowers."

Tam evinced not the slightest interest. After a moment he added: "There's a skirt gettin' out, can't see her face, she's that wrapped up in skins—will I open the door?"

"I suppose so."

A moment or two later, Inga Farrar rushed in, her arms laden with great sheaves of flowers which she promptly dropped in a fragrant heap on the couch, to extend both eager hands to Tam, who had risen and stood smiling, her long smoke-blue eyes narrowed by quizzical amusement.

"Still aggressively happy?" Tam laughed. "To look at you almost gives one faith in the marriage institution!"

Over Inga's passionately beautiful face swept a look of awe. "In a way, I owe it all to Leslie Carew—it was her life and death that cured Truxton of all social ambition. Now that the trial's over, we plan gypsying through the seven seas in the yacht he provided as a possible means of retreat in case they tried to arrest me."

"Poor Dorcas—she's the one doomed to pay through long years of prison. I sometimes wonder if the death-sentence isn't really more merciful in the end?"

"You heard that Lydia Chadwick is dead?"

Tam nodded. "Yes. Inspector McCoy wasn't wrong in predicting that she'd never live to endure a trial. And her husband—at least he and the Joker won't be free to guide any more victims along the path to drug slavery for some years to come."

The Hollow Tree Mystery
MADELON ST. DENIS

The MURDERS AT HILLSIDE
VIRGINIA RATH

THE RUMBLE MURDERS
Henry Ware Eliot, Jr.

THE BEACON HILL MURDERS

THE BACK BAY MURDERS

THE ROGER SCARLETT MYSTERIES
VOL. 1

Coachwhip Publications
CoachwhipBooks.com

MINNA BARDON

Eleanor Blake

MINNA BARDON

Coachwhip Publications
CoachwhipBooks.com

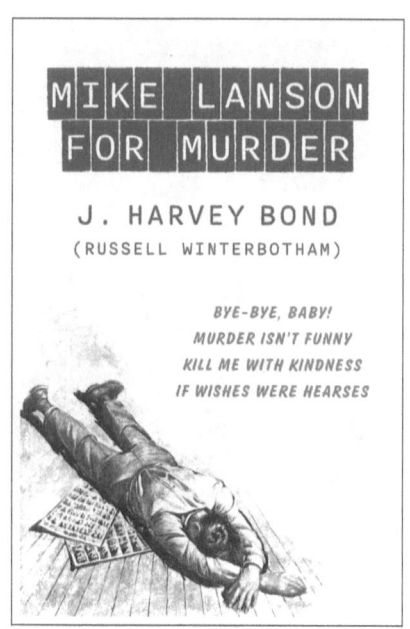

MIKE LANSON
FOR MURDER

J. HARVEY BOND

(RUSSELL WINTERBOTHAM)

BYE-BYE, BABY!
MURDER ISN'T FUNNY
KILL ME WITH KINDNESS
IF WISHES WERE HEARSES

MURDER ENDS THE SONG

ALFRED MEYERS

NARROW
GAUGE TO
MURDER

CAROLYN THOMAS

PATTERN
IN BLACK
AND RED

FARADAY KEENE

Coachwhip Publications
CoachwhipBooks.com

DEAD
WEIGHT
ADDISON
SIMMONS

DEATH
ON THE CAMPUS
ADDISON
SIMMONS

LOUIS F. BOOTH
THE BANK VAULT MYSTERY
BROKERS' END

MURDER
A LA
MODE
ELEANORE
KELLY
SELLARS
CLASSIC RED BADGE PRIZE MYSTERY

Coachwhip Publications
CoachwhipBooks.com

Coachwhip Publications
CoachwhipBooks.com

THE THING IN THE BROOK

PETER STORME

THE 13th GUEST by ARMITAGE TRAIL

Death at Windward Hill

Murder in the French Room

HELEN JOAN HULTMAN

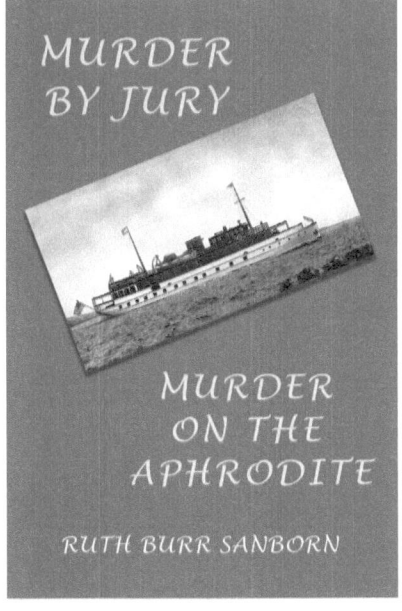

MURDER BY JURY

MURDER ON THE APHRODITE

RUTH BURR SANBORN

Coachwhip Publications
CoachwhipBooks.com

DRESSED TO KILL

Emma Lou Fetta

MURDER ON THE FACE OF IT

Emma Lou Fetta

MURDER IN STYLE

Emma Lou Fetta

THE FIRES AT FITCH'S FOLLY

KENNETH WHIPPLE

Coachwhip Publications
CoachwhipBooks.com

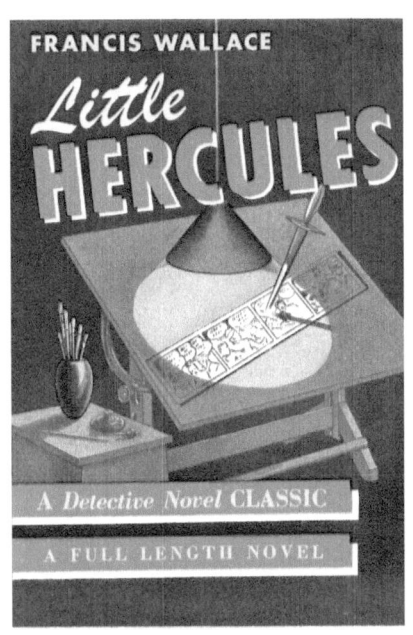

FRANCIS WALLACE

Little **HERCULES**

A *Detective Novel* CLASSIC

A FULL LENGTH NOVEL

MURDER AT THE KENTUCKY DERBY

CHARLES PARMER

MURDER ON THE BLUFF

ESTHER TYLER

3 DETECTIVES
MURDER ON THE RAILS
WHITECHURCH • THORNE • TORGERSON

Coachwhip Publications

CoachwhipBooks.com

www.ingramcontent.com/pod-product-compliance
Lightning Source LLC
Chambersburg PA
CBHW050525260626
47157CB00004B/1467